# BEHIND T

CU00349862

ROBIN MAUGHAM was born Robei
son of Frederic Maugham, 1st Visi
and nephew of the famous autho
at Eton and Cambridge, Maughai

decided to follow in his uncle's footsteps and pursue a career in literature.

Maugham served with distinction in World War II in North Africa, where he reportedly saved the lives of 40 men and sustained a head injury that resulted in blackouts. While convalescing from his wounds, Maugham wrote his first book, *Come to Dust* (1945), which drew on his war experiences. The book was praised by Graham Greene and sold well, convincing Maugham to continue writing full time. Over the next thirty years, Maugham would be one of England's most popular writers, publishing some twenty volumes of fiction and a dozen nonfiction works, including travel writing, biographies of his uncle, and the autobiography *Escape from the Shadows* (1972), which dealt frankly with the three "shadows" over Maugham's life: his father, his uncle, and his own homosexuality. Maugham was also a prolific playwright, writing scripts for stage, radio, and television.

Among his many works, highlights include the classic novella *The Servant* (1948), memorably filmed by Joseph Losey in 1963; *Line on Ginger* (1949), filmed as *The Intruder* (1953); *The Wrong People* (1967), a controversial novel dealing with pederasty and initially published pseudonymously, and *The Link: A Victorian Mystery* (1969), loosely based on the real-life Tichborne case.

On the death of his father in 1958, Maugham succeeded to the viscountcy, becoming the 2nd Viscount Maugham. His first speech in the House of Lords drew attention to the subject of human trafficking and led to a book on the subject, *The Slaves of Timbuktu* (1961). He traveled widely, living for ten years on the island of Ibiza, but towards the end of his life his health deteriorated due to diabetes and alcoholism. He died in Brighton in 1981.

*Cover*: The cover of this edition is a reproduction of the original jacket art by John Minton (1917-1957) from the first British edition, published in 1955 by Longmans. Minton was an extremely talented gay illustrator and painter whose career was cut tragically short by his suicide in January 1957. Among his other notable dust jackets were those for John Braine's *Room at the Top* (1957) and Martyn Goff's *The Plaster Fabric* (1957), both reproduced on the covers of the Valancourt reissues.

By Robin Maugham

Fiction
*The Servant* (1948)
*Line on Ginger* (1949)
*The Rough and the Smooth* (1951)
*Behind the Mirror* (1955)
*The Man with Two Shadows* (1958)
*The Slaves of Timbuktu* (1961)
*November Reef* (1962)
*The Green Shade* (1966)
*The Wrong People* (1967)
*The Second Window* (1968)
*The Link: A Victorian Mystery* (1969)
*The Last Encounter* (1972)
*The Barrier* (1973)
*The Black Tent and Other Stories* (1973)
*The Sign* (1974)
*Knock on Teak* (1976)
*Lovers in Exile* (1977)
*The Dividing Line* (1978)
*The Corridor* (1980)
*The Deserters* (1981)

Nonfiction, Biography and Travel
*Come To Dust* (1945)
*Nomad* (1947)
*Approach to Palestine* (1947)
*North African Notebook* (1948)
*Journey to Siwa* (1950)
*The Slaves of Timbuktu* (1961)
*The Joyita Mystery* (1962)
*Somerset and All the Maughams* (1966)
*Escape from the Shadows* (1972)
*Search for Nirvana* (1975)
*Conversations with Willie* (1978)

# BEHIND THE MIRROR

ROBIN MAUGHAM

VALANCOURT BOOKS

*Dedication*: For Kate

*Behind the Mirror* by Robin Maugham
First published by Harcourt, Brace and Company in April 1955
First U.K. edition published by Longmans in Oct. 1955
First Valancourt Books edition 2016

Published by Valancourt Books, Richmond, Virginia
http://www.valancourtbooks.com

ISBN 978-1-943910-24-3 (trade paperback)
Also available as an electronic book.

All Valancourt Books publications are printed on acid free paper
that meets all ANSI standards for archival quality paper.

Cover by John Minton. Reproduced by permission of the Royal
College of Art, London.

*Author's note*: There is no such company as Stonor Films in
Soho Square or anywhere else. There is no part of the Southern
Highlands called Aruna. All the characters in this novel are
imaginary, and imaginary names have been invented to suit them.
If by any chance the author has used the name of a living person
he apologizes.

ANTONIO   I am a tainted wether of the flock,
          Meetest for death: the weakest kind of fruit
          Drops earliest to the ground; and so let me:
          You cannot better be employ'd, Bassanio,
          Than to live still, and write mine epitaph.
                    *The Merchant of Venice.* Act IV, Sc. i.

# PART I

If you are late for a conference I believe it is best to walk in slowly and quietly with a look of mild surprise that those present have arrived early. I have known a man seem to be outrageously late for one of Stonor's film conferences because he bustled in, sweating and apologizing, when we had only been talking for five minutes.

I was nearly half an hour late when I reached the Stonor Building in Soho Square, and, for once, I acted on principle. I made myself walk slowly all the way down the long corridor. I smiled brightly at the secretaries in the outer office and slipped gently into the large white and gold conference room. As I sat down in one of the little red velvet armchairs drawn up around the huge mahogany desk I noticed with pleasure that Stonor's chair was empty. They were gossiping nervously. The conference had not yet started.

While I took my first "treatment" of the script out of my dispatch case I looked vaguely around the room. I knew them all, except for a short man in a black coat and striped trousers. I could not place him. He did not seem to belong to the little parish of Stonor Films. When he saw me looking at him he widened his mouth and parted his lips, revealing some very white false teeth, so I grinned back at him.

"You're late," Roy Nixon said, turning toward me.

I muttered something about the traffic in the late afternoon. Suddenly I wondered if I reeked of scent. Roy was looking at me suspiciously.

"Surely you know by now how long it takes to get across the Park?" he asked.

Roy had risen from the finance department to become Stonor's assistant. He was an eager red-haired man with a nose that twitched like a rabbit when he was excited. He was always dressed in a tightly fitting pin-striped suit of gray or blue which he enlivened with a carnation in season. To compensate for his ignorance about film technique he was over-enthusiastic and brisk. He adopted toward us the attitude of a keen nursery governess. Roy was sometimes irritating, but there was no doubt that he would go far on the business side.

"Surely you know by now how long it takes to get across the Park?" he repeated. "Surely . . ."

André Calmann silenced him with a wave of his heavy white hand.

"The important thing is that David is come," he said, beaming at me.

André Calmann was under contract to direct the picture we were working on. He had left Berlin a year before Hitler came into power and had made films in England ever since. He was an old hack, using tricks that he had been the first to discover but which were now outworn. He had an odd obsession. Into every film he introduced a fat woman laughing. Sometimes she laughed in the Sahara, sometimes on Chelsea Bridge or the slopes of the Matterhorn. No matter what the script said, there was the fat woman heaving with laughter. She was his talisman. But though Calmann had never again achieved the brilliance of his Berlin films he had never made a bad one, and at least he recognized a good story when he saw it – which was more than one could say for the rest of them. He was a heavily built man of about sixty, very carefully dressed, with a large gold seal dangling from his waistcoat pocket and a large cabochon ruby glowing on the little finger of his left hand. He was violently emotional and easily offended, but he was warmhearted and generous. He was the only one of them I really liked. Though he was an infinitely better technician than I was, we shared the same mixture of almost childishly romantic hope and cynical despair that is sometimes found in the industry. Perhaps, from across a desert of celluloid, hack called to hack.

"David, I am not quite happy about your opening sequences," he said, pulling his chair close to mine and speaking quietly so that the others should not hear. "This Daphne

Moore was a great actress. That is why we make a picture about her. I met her once, thirty years ago. She had temperament. Why are you afraid to show that she had temperament? You are making her too good, too kind."

"After all, she's supposed to be our heroine."

"So you want the audience to like her. But do you suppose they like a woman because she is good and kind? In their homes, perhaps yes. On the screen, no. No, David, you must show her weaknesses, her tempers, her jealousies. And if they give me the right actress I will make them love her for those very faults."

I could think of nothing to say. I nodded my head and handed him a cigarette. He had made me afraid that the last sequence I had prepared was hopelessly wrong.

While I was wondering if I could improvise a different ending the double doors at the far end of the room were flung open by a flustered secretary, and Louis Stonor walked quickly toward us. As he approached across the stretch of thick, fawn-colored carpet we all got up sheepishly – except Calmann, who nodded to him politely.

"Good afternoon, gentlemen," Stonor said as he settled himself behind the gleaming desk. "Are we ready to begin?"

"I think so, Sir Louis," Roy murmured, neatly placing a copy of my treatment in front of him.

Turning his head deliberately slowly Louis Stonor looked round at the semicircle of faces grouped beyond his desk. He was a squat man in his late fifties with broad shoulders that seemed to bulge out of his light blue suit. His face was white and very smooth, but the skin of his flat, wide nose was rough and pitted, as if it were of a different texture. He wore thick tortoise-shell spectacles, and as he looked around at us from behind the convex lenses, one eye swam slowly from side to side like a blue goldfish in a bowl, while the other eye stared straight ahead, for it was made of glass.

None of us really knew how Louis Stonor had lost his eye, but there were a dozen different stories current in the studio quite apart from the publicity department's official version that he had been hit by shrapnel in the Battle of the Somme. No one except Roy even pretended to believe the official version. Stonor's past was obscure, but it was known that in 1916 he had taken out a patent for a new type of soda-water bottle which had made him the small fortune he had used to invade the film world. He spoke in a guttural voice with a slight North Country accent. His ruthless methods had made him many enemies in the past. But there he now sat, powerful and benign, the executive head of one of the largest British film companies. He could now afford to be a man of good will. He could even indulge his odd streak of sentimentality. The orphan could be adopted, the lovers reunited, the sinner redeemed, the heroine rescued, the dying man consoled with a blessing. He could afford to let his glass eye stare fixedly at the box-office returns while the other eye roved slowly around in search of material to make the kind of film he thought was great.

He leaned toward me.

"Well, Dave, are you now ready to give us the last sequence?"

"I am," I said, trying to suppress the silly waves of fear I always felt before a race at school.

I took up my treatment.

"No, Dave, put that away," Stonor said quickly. "I want you to tell us the story in your own words. I want you to make me *see* what happens. And if I can really see it and like it, then we'll make it that way."

"Well," I began, "we've reached the stage . . ."

"Perhaps I had better recapitulate," Stonor interrupted. He was very fond of long words. "We've seen Daphne Moore's early life, her humble origin, her parents' struggle against poverty to give her the chance they didn't have, her first stage performance in Liverpool at the age of fifteen, her trials and temptations, her escape from seduction, her first success in London, and then in a quick montage sequence her rise to fame. We've seen her happy marriage to a wealthy industrialist, her loyalty to him and her love for her son Peter.

We've seen her courage when, learning halfway through the first night of 'Madam Rachel' that her husband is dead, she goes on to give a fine performance. We've seen her mourn the loss of her husband so much that she turns her back on the world and goes into retirement in the country to devote herself entirely to her son. So far we have had plenty of action. We have seen fear and courage, hatred and love. One thing we have not seen. Passion."

Stonor paused effectively. I happened to look at Calmann, who closed his left eye in a shameless wink.

"Passion is what the picture lacks so far," Stonor continued. "Now, Dave, let's hear how you propose to end the story of her life."

I stubbed out my cigarette and tried to look confident.

"Real life has been kind to us for once," I said. "What I'm going to tell you really did happen so far as I can discover. Daphne Moore retired in 1925. In 1927 a new character came into her life. He was a diplomat, and his name was Norman Hartleigh. He was thirty-eight years old. During the war he had obtained three years' leave of absence to serve with the Brigade of Guards in France, where he won a Military Cross. During the following ten years in the Foreign Office he had done surprisingly well for his age. He was considered one of the ablest men in the Service. To amuse himself in his spare time he had written a comedy called 'Wine for Caroline,' and his friends made him send it to Cole Edwards, the theatrical manager. Cole immediately saw that it was the perfect vehicle for Daphne Moore if only she could be persuaded to make a comeback. He went down to her house in Kent and begged her to read it. As he had hoped, she was delighted with it. Her son Peter had just gone to Eton. There was no reason why Daphne should not return to the London stage. She was a woman who made quick decisions. There and then she told Cole Edwards that she would play Caroline if various changes were made in the third act. Cole arranged for her to meet Norman for lunch at the Ritz three days later."

"You're not making me *see* any of this," Stonor said coldly.

"All that I've told you," I said, trying not to hurry my words, "can easily and briefly be established in a light scene between Daphne and Cole Edwards, who had always been hopelessly in love with her. The scene can take place in the garden of her country house with her son Peter interrupting them occasionally to ask what he should pack for school."

"Let's have her first meeting with this Norman," Stonor said.

"The Ritz is crowded. Cole Edwards at his usual corner table is chatting to Norman, who is half-nervous, half-amused. Daphne is late as usual. The camera favors Norman. He is slender but well-built, and elegantly dressed in a quiet way. He has an attractive, lean face, and a great sense of humor. He looks younger than his age. Suddenly several heads turn as Daphne sweeps in. Cole Edwards introduces the young author to the famous actress. And as their eyes meet for an instant they both remain motionless. For this is it. The *coup de foudre*. A simple thing. Love at first sight."

"Can you get that across, André?" Stonor asked.

Calmann let his gold seal drop against his waistcoat and opened his eyes.

"I have done so before," he replied flatly. "But I would like an exterior to follow."

"Cole Edwards leaves them after lunch," I said, "and Daphne walks with Norman across St. James's Park to the Foreign Office in the bright spring sunshine."

"Good," said Calmann, and began playing with his seal again.

Stonor looked at his watch. "Skip till we get to the night of the first rehearsal," he ordered.

"After the first rehearsal, Norman goes back to Daphne's flat in Chelsea to discuss alterations in the play. He was in love with her, but gently and adroitly she had stopped him declaring his love. Daphne had been in love before, but never so intensely. She was now afraid of the blind passion that consumed her. Remember she was ten years older than Norman."

"Let's have the scene," Stonor murmured quietly.

"They arrive in her flat. It is late, and her maid has gone to bed. Daphne pours out drinks and talks about the play. Norman begins to improvise changes in the love scene in the last act. As he speaks, suddenly Daphne realizes that his words are no longer dialogue for the play but the words of love he has always longed to speak to her. She tries to stop him, but the dam that controlled his passion has been broken. He takes her in his arms. And at last her arms go round his neck and their lips meet. Then with a little cry, she surrenders herself to the passion that has so tormented her."

"Now let's have the First Night," Stonor urged softly.

"For the last two months they have been inseparable, sharing each other's hopes and fears, living desperately in the present, so much in love that they did not know that their affair was common knowledge."

"Let's have the scene."

"The play is a terrific success. We see part of the love scene in the last act. Daphne gives a wonderful performance. We see the ovations, the curtain calls, the excited audience. We see the look that passes between Daphne and Norman when he appears to the shouts of 'author.' We dissolve to the party in Cole Edwards' flat after the First Night. Peter has been allowed up from Eton but is taken home early by Daphne's dresser. Daphne and Norman steal away together at two in the morning. They go back to her flat and he takes her in his arms. Close-up of her face. There are tears in her eyes. Desperately she forces herself to regain control so that he never knows that she has been crying. Then she moves away from him. Quietly, she tells him that they must part. She has heard that the scandal of their affair is damaging his career. In their happiness they have been too flagrant. Their long honeymoon must end.

"Norman looks at her steadily. 'There's only one way it can end,' he says. 'I love you more than anything in all the world. Daphne, will you marry me?' Daphne is standing by the fireplace with her back turned to him. In close-up we see how much his proposal means to her. Then she looks into the mirror which hangs over the chimney piece. In a big close-up we see for the first time the lines of age on her face. For an instant she turns around and looks at him. He still looks very young. 'And in ten years' time?' she asks. 'I'll love you as long as I live,' he answers.

"Then we see her look of resolve as she girds herself for the greatest performance of her career. When she now turns around to him her face appears hard and coarse. 'What makes you think I want to marry you?' she asks flippantly. 'I wanted a fling and I don't mind confessing I enjoyed it while it lasted. But can't you see what I'm trying to tell you as tactfully as I can? I'm tired of you, my dear. Just plain tired. And I want a change. You're not the only man in love with me, you know.'

"Her voice is strident, her features are contorted with contempt. Norman stares at her in horror. 'Hadn't you better take the hint and go?' she asks coldly. Without a word Norman turns and leaves the room. As he goes out of the door her whole expression changes and we see her love for him shining from her eyes. For a moment her resolve falters and she stretches out her arms toward the open door. In agony she stifles the cry that springs to her lips. Then we hear the sound of the front door closing, and in a gesture of supreme resignation her hands drop to her sides. And as the camera tracks toward her the music of our theme tune swells, and we know that at last she has fulfilled herself. She has had her greatest triumph as an actress. And in her complete self-sacrifice she has had her greatest triumph as a human being."

I leaned back and lit a cigarette. My hands were moist and trembling. I did not dare look at Calmann. I felt sick with shame. Halfway through my story I had realized I was handing out muck. It is sad enough to be middle-aged and second-rate; it is worse if you are constantly aware of the fact.

There was silence in the room. I knew that they were all waiting for Stonor to speak. I forced myself to look up at him. Slowly Stonor took off his spectacles. Then his hand fumbled in his breast pocket and produced a handkerchief. Fascinated, I stared at him as he wiped away a tear. Suddenly I felt like a child who has cheated his father. "Don't be taken in," I wanted to shout. "It's stale tripe I've served out to you. If only you give me the chance I'll produce something really good, something that is true." Then I remembered that I was not a creative artist, that I had little talent, that the reason I was paid sixty pounds a week was precisely because I could sometimes produce a sentimental story that made Stonor cry. If Stonor cried, the great film public might leave a thousand cinemas with a gulp of emotion. We were part of a vast industry. Why should we give the public wine if they wanted cocoa? If I could produce one good novel, one good story, even, I would starve rather than work on other people's books and outlines. But one must accept limitations and exploit such talent as one has. I have a flair for what entertains, and I write my scripts with a slight American accent that brings in dollars. I do not write my scripts as an artist because I am not an artist. I am technically accomplished and I have seldom had a failure at the box office. Why should I worry?

Thus, I repeated to myself the old exorcising phrases, my old incantations, but that particular afternoon they did not seem to work. I still felt ashamed.

Stonor had now recovered his poise.

"Gentlemen, before I give you my own opinion, I would like your criticisms," he said.

Roy's nose began to twitch violently.

"I just want to say I think it's absolutely first-rate," he said, blushing red and white like a beacon. Evidently he had noticed the tear.

"Desmond?"

We all turned toward Desmond Arles. He was a tall, slender man of forty, with a delicate face and long, wavy hair. He was dressed, deliberately, in a very old tweed jacket and dirty flannel trousers to show that he was "one of the boys." The effect was slightly marred by his Charvet tie. He was head of the scenario department. But for the war I would have had his job. Desmond had been excused from war service because of a stomach ulcer which had now miraculously healed.

"It's all right," he said in a despondent voice. "But I'm not sure the end isn't too sad, too downbeat for the box office."

As he spoke I heard the trumpet call to battle.

"I have prepared a list of ten films with downbeat endings that have appeared in the last three years and have made money at the box office," I said pleasantly, feeling better now that I could move into the attack. "Shall I read my list?"

"I can't imagine why you should call the end downbeat," Stonor said, blowing his nose angrily. "She has achieved the highest worldly success. And then, finally, she realizes the great spiritual truth – that only by sublimation of self can spiritual love be attained. What more do you want? Don't you agree, André?"

For a moment I thought that Calmann had gone to sleep. His eyes were shut, and he was breathing heavily. Then he gave a grunt and looked up at Stonor.

"I want a character," he said. "Perhaps she will become real to me when we begin to script."

"I'm certain she will," Stonor said. "What do you think, Eddie?"

Eddie Roach was head of the casting department. He was a brisk, efficient man with an extraordinary memory. If you wanted to know who played the second witch in "Macbeth" at the Bristol Rep in 1934 he could tell you.

"It's a perfect part for Nadia Browne," Eddie said, and then coughed nervously.

There was an awkward silence. I could feel the strain as they refrained from looking at me. Nadia had been my wife for five hectic years before the war. She had refused to have a child because she was afraid it would harm her career. In those days she was known in the press as a "starlet." I now realize that her career was all she cared about. While I was in Salerno she eloped with George Harrod, who had faced the perils of the west of Scotland to produce that valiant war film "Warrior's Return." I had since consoled myself with a ballet dancer called Wanda, who had made me late for the conference.

"We'll discuss the cast later," Stonor said crisply.

The green light on his desk had begun to flash. Angrily, Stonor reached for the green telephone and listened to a small frantic voice. Then he put down the receiver and turned to us.

"I'm afraid I haven't time for more criticisms," he said. "I'm late for a meeting of the Producers' Association. But before I go, can any one of you see any reason why we shouldn't go straight ahead and let Dave script the story with André in collaboration with the scenario department? Any objections?"

While Stonor's eye swam around the room no one spoke. Suddenly the short man in the black city suit leaned forward and cleared his throat and spoke for the first time.

"There is one possible objection," he said in a dry, high-pitched voice. "Daphne Moore, as we know, died in 1936. But Norman Hartleigh is still alive."

Then I remembered who the man was. He worked in the legal department, and his name was either Drake or Fowler.

"He must be pretty old," Desmond said.

"Only sixty. Remember he was ten years younger than she was."

"But we're making him a most sympathetic character," Stonor said. "What possible objection can he have?"

"You make him break the Seventh Commandment," Drake – I was sure it was Drake – said primly.

Calmann clasped his hands over his face, and his huge body began to shake in silent laughter.

"After the Youssupof case we can't be too careful," Drake continued. "If we portray on the screen the character of a person who is still alive, we must first get his permission in writing. We don't want a libel action for two hundred thousand pounds."

For some reason Calmann found this irresistibly funny. He covered his face with a highly colored silk handkerchief and gasped and snorted.

"We must go into this matter," Stonor said, glaring at Calmann. Then he turned to Drake. "I presume you've contacted Norman Hartleigh?"

"Not yet," said Drake.

"Why not? This film was on our schedule three months ago."

"He lives in Tanganyika."

"What difference does that make? Presumably you can still reach him by cable."

"I'm not certain about that."

"What do you mean, you're 'not certain'?"

"I cabled him nine weeks ago and I've still had no reply."

"The cable probably went astray. What's the use of *one* cable?"

"Precisely," Drake nodded. "That is why I have sent him no less than ten cables, reply paid. But I've had no answer."

"He may be dead."

"So I thought. I therefore got in touch with his literary agent, who gave me the address of the bank in Dar-es-Salaam where Mr. Hartleigh has an account. A week ago I cabled to the bank manager. I received a reply this morning."

"Well?" Stonor asked impatiently.

"Mr. Hartleigh cashed a check last Monday."

Drake leaned back in his chair and folded his delicate hands as if to protect them.

"Perhaps your cables never reached him."

"At least one of them did."

"How can you be certain?"

"Because I took the precaution of sending a copy of it to the bank."

"Then why do you suppose you have had no reply from him?"

"I can think of only two reasons. Either he is completely indifferent to the whole project or he dislikes the prospect of a film being made about the woman he loved."

Desmond Arles got up and took a cigarette from the open silver box on the desk.

"Do you really need to use Hartleigh as a character?" he asked. "Couldn't Daphne Moore just as well have fallen in love with a promising young lawyer or an army officer with a great career ahead of him?"

Stonor tapped his notes angrily.

"The fact remains that she fell in love with a young diplomat, and we're making the story of her life," he said. "It's a true story we're telling. I want it to ring true. As soon as we begin changing characters we shall distort values. I want the real thing or nothing."

"Then I think it would be a great mistake to move on to script stage before we've got the Hartleigh matter cleared up," Desmond said.

Stonor banged his fist on the desk. He was trembling with anger.

"This is just what I have to complain about," he shouted. "Why wasn't I told about this hitch? Why wasn't I kept informed? This delay may affect our whole schedule. What are you all paid for? Why are you here today? It's unbelievable that I wasn't informed."

Drake unclasped his hands.

"I sent you a memorandum on the matter three weeks ago and a further memorandum last Monday," he said.

For a moment Stonor was baffled. He lowered at us in silence. Then he banged the desk again.

"Memorandums," he cried. "What's the good of memorandums? Why wasn't I *told?* This wretched Hartleigh man can delay us indefinitely." Stonor turned toward Drake.

"What precisely do we need to get from Hartleigh? You say 'his permission,' but what does that mean? Do we have to get his agreement to every page of the script?"

"It would be sufficient to get his agreement to the treatment."

"Is he rich? Does money mean anything to him?"

"I don't know," Drake said.

"Then get on to his agent and find out. Why has he got an agent? What is he doing in Tanganyika? I thought you said he was a diplomat," Stonor said, staring at me accusingly.

"He retired from the Foreign Office in 1928," I said. "I believe he wrote two travel books."

"They can't bring him in much money. Have you sent him an outline of the film?"

"Airmail. Three weeks ago," Drake replied.

Stonor got up from his desk and walked over to the window and stared down at the wet November evening. Then he snapped his fingers and turned around to us.

"This delay means we shall have to revise our whole schedule," he said. "We'll go ahead with 'The Crimson Doll' and make 'Daphne Moore' in the summer of 1950. So far as this Hartleigh man is concerned there's only one thing to do. Someone must go out to Tanganyika and see him personally. Letters and cables are no good with a man like that. He's got to be personally convinced that our film is going to do credit to the memory of the woman he loved. Desmond, who can we spare?"

I stared at my cigarette and held my breath. I had planned to take Wanda to Kitzbühl for Christmas. The last place I wanted to visit was Tanganyika.

"If we're going ahead with 'The Crimson Doll' why don't we send David?" Desmond suggested, after a pause.

"That's right," Stonor said. "We can send David."

"What about the script?" I asked. "It's going to take all of three months."

"You needn't be away for long. Have you ever been to East Africa?"

"Never."

"You may get the idea for a film. Look around a bit. Go on a safari. Meet the people out there. That last African picture did great business on circuit. You can kill two birds with one stone. But first, get this Hartleigh man fixed. After all, it's your own treatment. Tell him the picture will be made in perfect taste. Tell him he'll be proud of it. I don't for a moment suppose he'll be awkward, but if he is, offer him money."

"How much?" I asked.

"Start at five hundred and go up to a thousand if necessary. But use your common sense. You'd better go and see the finance department. I'll send them a note in the morning. You can leave next week."

Stonor looked at his watch and moved toward the door. Roy got up quickly and followed him.

"Thank you, gentlemen," Stonor said.

"Just supposing Norman Hartleigh refuses a thousand?" I asked as Roy opened the door for him.

"He won't," Stonor said as he walked out. "Good night, gentlemen."

The conference was over.

## PART II

I sat in a wicker chair on the terrace of the club in Dar-es-Salaam waiting gloomily for a Mr. Partridge, who was the manager of the bank where Norman Hartleigh had an account. I had arrived by plane on Friday evening and discovered that Partridge had gone up to Mombasa for the weekend, taking his assistant with him. I had spent two sticky days wandering around vaguely in search of material for a film story. The town would provide the perfect background for a really sordid murder, I decided as I sipped my whisky.

For all the tropical beauty of palms and glittering sea and exotic flowers, Dar-es-Salaam was a disturbing, nerve-racking place where two worlds mingled and yet did not meet. By the harbor and along the water front Africans of all ages, looking far smaller and shabbier than I had imagined, lounged and stared and spat. Connecting this area with the main street were the rickshaw boys, depressingly ugly and squat, straining their bow legs to pull forward their white cargo from the north – overfed tourists, red-faced planters with thick hairy thighs, pallid, weedy experts from the Ministry of Food concerned with ground nuts, spruce officials in their white shorts and white stockings. Peering without interest through their dark spectacles, watching dispassionately the sweat trickling down black flesh, the Europeans were hauled to their bars and clubs and hotels. In the small main street, Acacia Avenue, one became aware of people from a third world profiting from the gap between the other two. Most of the little shops were owned by Indians, obsequious and plump, with dishonest eyes. Clever and hard-working, they were acquiring land. Here, the crafty might inherit the earth.

The heat was almost unbearable. All day long the sun beat down fiercely on the burning pavement of the streets, and one's body stirred uneasily, yearning for darkness. But it was as if the sun drew away the air when at last it sank. The nights were stifling. While the electric fans wheezed and groaned in the darkness of my bedroom in a recently built hotel, I would turn over on soaked sheets, panting for breath. Only toward dawn, when a faint breeze was released from the horizon, was it possible to sleep until the noise and heat of a new day. I had heard that Norman Hartleigh lived somewhere up in the Southern Highlands. No one but a fool would live in Dar-es-Salaam for pleasure at this time of the year.

I looked up from my drink. A neatly dressed short man of about fifty was approaching my table.

"My name's John Partridge," he said. "You wanted to see me. Let's go to the bar. You get served quicker there."

We wandered into the long barroom and ordered two whiskies from the African waiter. Partridge had a small mustache and delicate girlish hands which were carefully manicured. He smelled faintly of antiseptic, like a dentist.

"I believe you wanted to see me about Norman Hartleigh," he said. "What do you want to know about him?"

"As much as you can tell me," I replied, and explained to him briefly about the film. As he listened, he kept touching his little mustache as if to make sure it was still there.

"I'm afraid there's not much I can tell you," he said, when I had finished. "I only met Hartleigh once, and that was when he first came out here three years ago. But he's certainly alive."

"Where does he live?"

"He bought a farm property in the Southern Highlands about fifty miles west of Aruna. I can give you the address."

"Does he live there alone?"

Partridge hesitated.

"No," he said after a pause.

"Is he married?"

"He's a bachelor, so far as I know."

"Does he run the farm himself?"

"No. His friend is the manager."

"His friend?"

Partridge pursed his lips together and looked at his glass in disapproval.

"A young man by the name of William Wayne. They have a joint account at our local branch."

"Where did they meet?"

"I can only tell you that they arrived out here together. Some people thought it rather odd."

A tall gray-haired man in a gabardine suit was leaning against the bar a few feet away from us. With interest I had watched him drink three large whiskies in ten minutes. His long bony fingers trembled as he stretched forward to clutch each new glass. Suddenly he turned around and stared at Partridge.

"Are you talking about Norman Hartleigh?" he asked.

Partridge nodded his head. "Yes, Sir Owen," he said with a little smirk.

"No friend of yours, I hope," the tall man said, staring at me with protuberant blue eyes.

"I've never met him," I replied coldly.

"Allow me to introduce," Partridge said quickly. "Mr. David Brent, Sir Owen Dilke. Sir Owen has got one of the biggest sisal estates in the country," he added as if that explained everything.

With an effort Dilke managed to produce a cigarette from his gold case.

"And I can tell you one man who will never be allowed on

it," he said. "If I had my way Hartleigh would be flung out of the country. A person like that is a menace to any decent community."

"In what kind of way?" I asked gently.

"It was bad enough when he turned up here with a young man whose accent you could cut with a knife. But in these days of groundnuts one can't be too particular. Some people thought the worst, of course, but I never agreed with them. You can't have it both ways, or can you? Because then came the young native girl."

The long glass quivered as he raised it to his lips. I stared at him in bewilderment. I felt I was losing track of the conversation.

"Then came the young native girl," Dilke repeated.

"I never knew there was a young native girl," Partridge murmured, patting his mustache.

"Fortunately very few people did, though Hartleigh was flagrant enough about it. He picked her up in the native quarter here. Well, that wasn't so bad. I mean, if a man wants to go off at night in a rickshaw and visit their filthy hovels and find himself a girl and risk getting some ghastly disease, well, good luck to him. If he's careful he won't be seen driving in or driving out. But this fellow picks up the girl and has the effrontery to take her to a restaurant – a restaurant on the main street, mind you."

"Perhaps he wanted to write a story about her," I said. "After all, he is a writer."

The bulging blue eyes stared at me with contempt.

"When the girl couldn't speak a word of English and he couldn't speak a word of Swahili? I can see you're new to these parts. Do you realize that in South Africa the man would have been thrown into jail?"

"But we're not in South Africa," I said.

"No. But we've still got our standards – as you will find out if you live here any time. And one or two of us felt it our duty to warn Hartleigh to clear out of the town – which he did pretty quick."

Dilke looked at me triumphantly and then glanced down at his glass, which was empty.

"What about a round of drinks?" he asked.

Partridge hastily ordered three whiskies. Once again the bony fingers trembled across the polished bar like the claws of a dockside crane and lifted the glass.

"He went and buried himself somewhere in the Southern Highlands," Dilke continued. "No one down here has heard of him much since."

He paused and leaned forward to us slowly and nodded his head three times.

"But I can tell you this," he whispered. "The young native girl went with him. I've heard that on the highest authority. She's still there."

Dilke connected the rim of his glass with his lips and tilted back his head. Then he lowered his glass and focused his eyes on my face.

"Did I gather from your conversation that you were going to visit the man?" he asked.

"Yes."

"Well, there's no accounting for tastes," Dilke said, and shuffled out of the bar before I could think of a suitable reply.

2

As the train from Dar-es-Salaam to Dodoma climbed gradually away from the coast, the country opened like a shell, and I began to feel a little happier. Even the ceiling of the sky seemed higher, and soon all around lay spread the vastness of Africa. Toward evening the air became wonderfully cool.

Sitting opposite me in the dining car was a pleasant-looking man in his late thirties with thick brown hair and a badly sunburned face. I peered cautiously at the book he was reading. It was a government report on the tsetse fly, and he was reading it avidly. At the next table two couples were playing liar dice on the tablecloth. I finished the thick soup and looked out at the moon shining over mountain crests that looked thin and brittle as if made of cardboard. I began to wonder again what kind of man Norman Hartleigh was.

When I had first started my treatment I had thought of Hartleigh as a lean romantic type, warmhearted yet cool and efficient, a man who was passionately in love with Daphne Moore yet was sufficiently worldly and detached to allow her to sacrifice their love for the sake of his career. Then I discovered that within a year of the famous first night of his play, Norman Hartleigh had retired from the Foreign Office and had left England for good. He had never written another play, but he had produced two books of travel, one set in Syria, the other in Abyssinia. Though his books had not been successful in England, they had established his reputation as a writer of importance among various international critics. From the books I gained a different impression of him. Though he kept himself well in the background, a definite character emerged from his writing – an ascetic, rather shy man, who looked out upon the vanity of mankind with a tolerant smile on his lips. Such a man might well forsake his career and withdraw from the world to find peace in his own soul. I had imagined him dressed in an old flannel suit with frayed but clean linen, sitting alone in his quiet study looking out over the blue hills of some distant land with the Bhagavad-Gita on his knees.

This second vignette of Hartleigh had been ripped to pieces in my mind when I heard about young William Wayne with the Cockney accent. The study now became transformed into a living room with pastel green walls. Hartleigh now wore a plum-colored velvet dinner jacket, and, if there was any book on his lap, it was written by Gide. This third picture would in its turn be destroyed by the young native girl, if she existed. Hartleigh was now all bits and pieces in my mind, as if I were looking at him through a kaleidoscope.

The African waiter put two large steaks on the table and went away to fetch some vegetables. The pleasant red-faced man opposite smiled at me shyly.

"Are you new to these parts?" he asked.

I nodded, wondering what in particular had revealed me as a newcomer.

"I thought so from the way you looked at the steaks," he said. "You don't get steaks that size in dear old England nowadays. Going up to the Southern Highlands?"

"Yes, for a while."

"It's the best part of the country. We've got a little place up there. You must pay us a visit. The wife gets bored stiff at times. Our nearest neighbors are more than twenty miles away."

We talked together for the rest of the evening as the train chuffed slowly up the gradient toward Dodoma.

I was lucky to have met him. Though he was diffident by nature, he enjoyed talking as only those do who have lived for long in remote places, and I liked his quiet voice with its faint burr and his blue wide-set eyes. His name was Tim Curry and he was forty, I discovered. He had bought a small farm near Aruna before the war; he had met his wife when he returned to London to join up; the farm was now prospering; if all went well they would be able to afford to send their two children to school in England.

"What about you?" he asked presently.

For several reasons I had decided that it was wiser not to mention my little mission to Hartleigh. I explained that I had come out to look around for a film story.

"If you want to get about in the Southern Highlands you'll need a car," he said. "Why not buy one in Dodoma? But I must warn you that my advice is highly biased," he added, grinning at me mischievously. "I had to leave our truck for my wife to use on the farm. It's a two-day journey up from rail-head by bus, and it just drives me nuts. If you buy an old car of sorts we can drive up together. You can always sell it again."

Stonor's finance department had paid a large sum of money into the bank at Dodoma for me to draw on for my salary and expenses. I even had a checkbook. Before we parted that evening for our respective sleepers we decided that I should buy an old Chevrolet or a Ford pick-up.

## 3

The train arrived at Dodoma at seven the next morning. Tim Curry, looking fresh and clean, leaped down onto the platform and found two native boys to carry our luggage into the small hotel opposite the station.

"Breakfast first," he said firmly. "Never buy a car on an empty stomach."

As we walked in, the manager was saying wearily to three dusty travelers: "No. We've got no rooms free. Not even one."

"If I had capital to spare I'd invest it in the hotel business and eat up the profits," Tim said as we sat down at a free table in the crowded dining room. "Now what shall we start with? Papaws, mangoes or avocado pears? What about some eggs to follow? Eggs five cents each, a whole chicken only a shilling, meat forty cents a pound – less than sixpence. I bet that startles you after living in England."

After breakfast we strolled through the narrow streets between single-storied mud huts until we came to a grimy garage owned by an obscenely fat, middle-aged Indian called Nushki. In a corner of the long shack we found a battered Chevrolet which Tim inspected carefully. He then winked at me furtively and announced in a loud voice that the car was a complete wreck, worth perhaps a hundred pounds. Nushki rushed out furiously from behind a Ford truck where he had been lurking and said that he had refused an offer of three hundred only yesterday. For half an hour they argued with unconcealed loathing. Sometimes Nushki's bitterness would defeat his English and he would break into passionate Swahili. Suddenly they both smiled and shook hands warmly, and Tim told me that I had bought the car for two hundred and must give Nushki a check on the local bank.

"What about registration and insurance?" I asked, taking out my checkbook.

"Don't worry. Nushki will fix all that. You're not in England now," Tim said, patting Nushki on the back.

Nushki looked up at me with wide, liquid eyes.

"Have you money in the bank?" he asked.

"Surprisingly enough, I have."

"That is all right," he said, flashing his gold teeth at me as he smiled. "I know you are a great gentleman when you come in. I trust you completely. I trust every English gentleman. Please write your name on this piece paper and I make out receipt."

I wrote down my name in block letters and the name of the film company. Nushki seized the paper, rushed out of the shack, and disappeared around the corner.

"Now where's he gone?" I asked.

Tim grinned at me. "To telephone through to the bank, of course. He doesn't trust English gentlemen all *that* far."

Though the old Chevrolet rattled and squeaked on the way back to the hotel, the engine sounded healthy, and Tim was pleased. Outside the hotel Tim said that he had some chores to do before we left, so I suggested he use the car. He looked at me and laughed.

"You won't keep that car long if you go lending it to strangers," he said. "This is a rough country, I keep telling you. How do you know that I won't head straight for Nairobi and never be seen again? How do you know?"

"I don't," I said, handing him the keys, "but I can make a fairly good guess. How long will you be?"

"Meet you here in an hour," he said, and waved to me as he drove away.

I had nothing in particular to do, and I wandered idly along the dusty street, past the gray Protestant cathedral with its fat dome, toward the market place which was more photogenic. Hordes of natives were squatting around the sheds which sheltered their merchandise. Standing apart watch-

ing them were their women, smooth-skinned young African
girls with their bodies swathed in brightly colored lengths of
cotton made in Manchester and their hair twisted tightly into
plaits so that their heads looked corrugated like the roofs of
the sheds. I tried to discover some expression in their faces as
they gazed on their men. Was it possessiveness or devotion
or dislike? I couldn't tell. Surveying both men and women
impassively were African policemen, very clean and erect in
smart khaki uniforms, trained into an outward show of disci-
pline by the protective power of a distant land.

Away from the market place ran parallel rows of dingy
mud huts with natives sprawling against the walls in the dirt
outside while naked pot-bellied children played around them
in the street. Only the little girls in their gay print dresses
seemed to have any vitality. Most of the natives looked at
me apathetically. But sometimes I thought I saw a flicker of
resentment in their eyes.

For a while I stood still in this dun-colored assembly of
huts. A drunken native shambled down the street calling out
"jambo" in greeting to each person he met. An old deformed
woman staggered past carrying a square can of water on her
head. It was all good background material if only I could find
the right story.

Then I looked up to the end of the street. Framed by the
drab fronts of the huts on either side was wild, open country,
stretching toward craggy blue hills strewn with boulders shining pure white in the sunshine. Two hundred miles beyond
those hills in country still higher and wilder lay Norman
Hartleigh's home. I wondered what he thought about Africa.
Did he live immersed in his remote farm, ignoring the trou-
bles and dirt and disease of those who lived below? Or did
he believe, like Tim Curry, that in return for the profit they
made in East Africa the Europeans should improve the health
of the natives, bring them security, and educate them toward
self-government. I wondered what I believed myself. Perhaps
I would not stay in Tanganyika long enough to find out.

★

When I returned to the hotel, Tim was standing beside the Chevrolet and our luggage was packed neatly in the back.

"Would you like me to drive?" he asked. "I love driving and you probably want to look around at the country."

"Let me know if you get tired."

"Don't you worry. I will."

Slowly the car clattered away from the town toward the tall hills in the distance. Where the road was not deeply rutted it had been worn away by the rains of the previous season into shallow depressions which made the car shudder. Less than five miles from Dodoma we passed one of the railway company's buses, which had broken down. Two natives, covered in grease, were asleep in the shade of the hood.

"Now are you glad you bought a car?" Tim asked.

Presently he began to talk diffidently about his struggle before the war to turn the barren land he had bought into a good property. He spoke simply and vividly. Stonor would have liked his style. I could almost *see* Tim with his native boys clearing the ground, contouring their first field by digging a ditch with a bank behind it to stop water flowing down, making bricks from the reddish mud they had found near the swamp, covering them with straw to dry in the sun. And while I listened I gazed out of the window at the broad plain spread around us, admiring the squat yet tall baobab trees with their naked menacing branches and the light green thorn bushes sprinkled over the flat red soil, childishly thrilled when I saw a gazelle bounding away to cover or a guinea hen scuttling in the undergrowth. I began to feel I was moving toward a new world.

At three o'clock we stopped in the shade of a tree with a lonely native shop beside it and ate the food Tim had brought and sipped tea from the shop, watched inquisitively by hordes of native children and by three stringy Masai warriors, indolent, tough and half-naked, leaning proudly on the shafts of their long shining spears – just waiting for a camera.

The sun beat down fiercely on the dusty road, and the car was stifling when we started again on our long journey. Tim had firmly refused my offer to drive. He was now silent, and I had the impression there was something worrying him.

"I'm sorry we can't ask you to stay," he blurted out suddenly. "But while the children are at home we've got no spare room."

I looked at him. His face was redder than usual with embarrassment. It was the lack of a spare room that had been worrying him. Quickly I explained that I never dreamed he would ask me to stay and that already I owed him gratitude for all his help.

"If you've got a room it's usual to ask people to stay in these parts," he said curtly. "As it is, you won't be able to stay at our little club because the only three guest rooms are occupied. The best place for you is the Rest House at Aruna. It's run by a grand old woman known as Ma Bolting. You'll like her. Everyone does. And one of her little bungalows is always empty."

"How many properties are there in the Aruna district?" I asked, hoping to hear something about Hartleigh.

"Very few. Don't expect Aruna to look like Sussex. We've each of us got between five and ten thousand acres. But most of the land's useless except for light grazing. In the Aruna part of the Southern Highlands there are only four properties and they lie roughly in diamond formation. At the south end of the diamond there's Ma Bolting's property where you'll be staying. Her husband died ten years ago, leaving her a tidy sum he'd made in the Lupa gold field. She runs the Rest House mainly because she likes company, so far as I can see, though she gets few enough guests. Then, on the west side there's Barry Leyton's property which is the biggest in the district."

"What's he like?"

"Some people find him a bit difficult, but his wife is a honey. Mary Leyton's one of the sweetest women I know. Then to the north there's our place, and to the east there's a farm owned by a man called Norman Hartleigh."

I had got there at last.

"What's he like?" I asked casually.

Tim was silent for a moment. I almost laughed when I found I was holding my breath.

"He's an odd sort of man. I can't pretend to understand him. He doesn't go about much. You'll hardly ever see him at the club. I've got nothing against him. He's always been perfectly civil to me. But my wife can't stand the sight of him."

"Any particular reason?"

"He's got a farm manager, a boy called Bill Wayne. Often a farm manager has a cottage of his own, but these two live in the same house and take their meals together. They go off on trips up and down the coast together, and they always share a bedroom in the hotels. And you know what women are. They always think the worst."

Tim was staring straight ahead at the road, his face rigid with embarrassment.

"I'm telling you this because if you're coming to our parts you'll soon find out for yourself," he said. "In a small community like ours women have got nothing else to do when they meet but gossip."

"What do you believe yourself?"

"I believe it's all nonsense, for two very good reasons. First, because Bill's hopelessly in love with Mary Leyton. Whenever he can find an excuse, he takes their farm truck and drives off to meet her. He's a fool, mind you, because if those two started anything Barry Leyton would be a dangerous customer."

Again Tim was silent. He changed gear for a dip in the road. I lit a cigarette and handed it to him.

"You said there were two reasons," I said gently.

"Yes. But I oughtn't to tell you the second reason. I only found it out by chance from a native boy who'd tried to get a job at Hartleigh's place. If my wife knew she'd throw a fit and then make a beeline for the club to tell the gossip circle. But I reckon I can trust you."

"Yes. You can now," I said.

"Well, here's the second reason," Tim said. "Hartleigh's

got a young native girl living on his place and she goes with him."

"Is that so very awful?"

"The club lot would think so. You see, quite apart from the question of color, he's sixty and the girl's only sixteen. But if you ask me, I don't think it so awful. The girl comes from the filthiest quarter of Dar-es-Salaam. At worst she'd now be spending all day and all night long lying on her back in a native brothel. At best she'd have been bought by some rickshaw boy who'd saved up a bit of money or stolen it, and he'd use her like an animal and beat her when he was drunk. At least she's now well treated. At least she's not bruised and whipped. I've had to see some of the girls on my place after their men have got drunk and lammed into them. It's not a pretty sight."

Tim threw his cigarette out of the window and brushed away a fly from his damp forehead.

"It's time I came clean," I said.

"You're not a journalist, I hope?"

"Worse than that. I write films – I told you."

While the car springs chattered over the wrinkles worn in the surface of the road by the wind and rain, I explained to him why I had come to see Norman Hartleigh.

"Good luck to you," he said when I had finished.

"Why do you think he didn't answer our cables?"

"Couldn't be bothered to, I suppose."

"Do you think he'll have any objection to the film?"

"Why should he – as long as you've made her the heroine and him the hero?"

"Is he well off?"

"He's not poor. He must have some private means because that farm of his doesn't make a penny. But to judge from appearances he's certainly not rich. You can see for yourself tomorrow."

"Shouldn't I write to him first?"

Tim chuckled.

"We don't write letters to each other up there. They take too long to get delivered. We just drive over and call."

"What's the best time to call?"

"Toward sundown if you want a drink," Tim said, laughing. "Light me another cigarette, will you?"

Gradually the country changed as we climbed higher. The slopes of the blue hills were now thickly wooded. An hour later we reached the foot of the steep escarpment that led up the mountainside to Iringa. Tim changed down into second gear.

"Beware of elephants," he said. "And I'm not being funny. They've knocked a car right over the precipice before now. If you're in a car and you meet an elephant, never switch off your engine. Put the gear into neutral and accelerate like mad. The noise of an engine revving up frightens him off. But you can blow your horn fit to deafen him, and he'll take no notice."

"Thanks for the tip," I said. I was feeling a long way from Soho Square. A thousand feet below us we could now see the vast plain we had crossed. The air was fresh and cold. At last we had reached the Southern Highlands.

The rest of the journey remains confused in my mind, probably because I was tired. Vaguely, I can remember dining in Iringa and leaving in darkness, the headlights picking out the milestones so that I could say to myself: "Only sixty more miles, only fifty miles." Then, I must have dozed awhile, for it was with a start that I heard Tim say: "Here's the turning."

The car lurched up a narrow track toward a clump of trees. I rubbed my eyes and lit a cigarette. Dotted among the trees were the lights of three buildings. Here was the Aruna Rest House. We drove up to the largest of the bungalows and got out stiffly.

"We may find Ma Bolting still in the bar," Tim said.

We walked into a room paneled in dark wood like an English pub. Alone behind the bar, cleaning a pewter mug, was a buxom gray-haired woman of about sixty.

"Look what the cat's brought in," she cried when she saw Tim.

Tim walked up to the bar and kissed her on both cheeks.

"How's Ma?" he asked.

"As well as can be expected," she said. "Now, you can't make love to me all night. Introduce me to your friend. Where's your manners? Left them behind in Dar, I suppose."

"This is David Brent, and he's come to stay with you."

She put on her spectacles to look at me.

"Well, that might be worse," she said placidly. "For him, I mean, of course. I don't count around these parts, as you'll soon discover, young man."

"He's not young, he's forty," Tim said. "Same as I am."

"Forty's young enough for me," she said. "Now what about a round on the house to welcome the stranger? Wait just one moment. I must tell the boy to get your room ready."

She opened the door behind her and shouted out: "Sha-bete!" While she was pouring out our drinks a plump little boy sidled in grinning. Mrs. Bolting spoke to him rapidly in Swahili.

"N'dio, Memsaab," he said, and turned to go.

"And don't be long about it or I'll tan your backside," she called after him in English. "Lazy little beggar," she said, turning back to us, "but he means well. Now what about a game of liar dice for the next round? You can tell me all the news from Dar while we play. But don't you think I'm going to stay open all night for you again, Tim Curry, because I'm not. You're both tired silly and I've got work to do. Where'd that damn boy put the dice?"

For a while I lay in my comfortable bed watching the firelight playing up and down the whitewashed walls. Tim had driven home in my car. He was coming back to return it in the morning. I would drive over to see Hartleigh toward sundown.

I closed my eyes. I felt tired but happy.

# 4

When I awoke the sun was streaming through a gap in the chintz curtains of my little room, and it was noon. I shouted for Shabete. Ten minutes later he appeared with hot water. In dumb show I explained to him that I didn't want breakfast. I shaved and dressed hurriedly and walked out onto the veranda. There was no one about.

The scrub around the Rest House was dry and withering, scorched brown by the sun though the air was crisp and cool. To the south I could see the great plain below with its broad spaces dotted with clumps of trees like an English park rolling gently away into the distance toward a green swamp. Ten miles beyond the far side of that swamp lay Norman Hartleigh's farm.

Keeping a sharp lookout for snakes, I strolled down the gentle slope. The sky seemed very far away, and what I can only describe as the "openness" of the landscape was exhilarating and rather disturbing. The ground was like a rock underfoot. The rains were long overdue. There was a tenseness in the sharp brittle grass and the hard-baked earth as if the whole plain were craving moisture. Some of the stunted dry trees had pushed out violent red flowers from the ends of their twisted naked branches, as if in protest. I passed a herd of native cattle, thin, mangy-looking creatures with humps on their backs, searching vainly for pasture. The herd was tended by a tiny boy who called out "Jambo" in a high treble voice and waved at me cheerfully. Then, to my left, I saw that the scrub had been cut down to form a broad track that ran across the plain from the corner of the swamp to the top of the hill. This was one of the firebreaks I had heard about. The clearing was five yards wide and extended for several miles. Months of labor must have been needed to make it. I could understand now why natives made a god of rain.

When I returned from my walk I found Mrs. Bolting alone in the bar playing darts.

"At eleven this morning you were sleeping so soundly that we let you lie," she said. "But you missed quite a party. First, Tim came out to bring back your car. Then Susan, his wife, had to come as well in their truck to drive him back. And on top of all that the Leytons dropped in, and they've asked you to dinner tonight."

"But I don't even know them."

"You soon will. Tim said you had a nice face and I said you hadn't pinched any silver to date, so they asked you to dinner. Any time after eight."

"I was going to call on Norman Hartleigh."

"So you shall. You've got a car, haven't you? Take a drink off him at sundown. Take six drinks off him if you get the chance. You'll still have time to get to Mary and Barry for dinner. I'll draw you one of my famous maps, then you can't go wrong."

"Are you sure Hartleigh will be there?"

"Of course he'll be there. Bill Wayne called in to see me yesterday. What about playing darts for a glass of beer before lunch?"

An hour before sunset I was driving along the uneven road that led to Norman Hartleigh's farm. In the evening light, each hillock and tree stood out in sharp detail with an intense clarity. I felt as if my eyes had been cleaned and polished like a lens – so vividly could I see the landscape spread around me. A reedbuck loped slowly across the scrub. From behind a bank a swarm of vultures rose, flapping their ungainly wings with slow angry gestures. Bluebirds flashed in the straggling bushes. I was aware of it all, but I was thinking about Norman Hartleigh. I tried to douse my excitement. I kept telling myself that I was only going to find a seedy old wreck, a retired civil servant who had once written a successful play and two good books, a man of so little consequence to the world that people in London thought he was dead. The fact remained: I was now three miles away from the object of my journey.

I had reached the long dip marked on Mrs. Bolting's map. The turning appeared to be halfway up the rise. And there, nailed to a tree trunk, was the jagged side of a packing case with the word Imunda written on it. The car clattered along a narrow bumpy track running across the plain. Then, as the open ground began to slope down toward the valley, I saw the house. It was shaped like the letter H, with a light brown thatched roof and whitewashed walls. From a distance it looked trim and unreal, like a child's hut made from icing sugar and marzipan. But when I drove closer I saw that it was less neat and clean than I had supposed. The thatch was untidy and the walls were discolored.

Apart from a small yard between the two wings of the house there seemed no place to turn a car. I stopped on the track and walked down the slope. A tall, thin native boy of about forty appeared from an outhouse and greeted me.

"Jambo, Bwana."

"Jambo," I replied idiotically, feeling like a character in a second feature. "Where is your Bwana?"

He signed to me to follow him. We walked around the corner of the main building. At the far end of a long veranda a man of about sixty was sitting in a wicker chair. There was no doubt. This was Norman Hartleigh.

He did not notice our arrival. He was staring toward the distant hills. The sun had begun to set, and a long shadow was creeping over the plain. The boy turned back into the house and left me alone, watching him. He was leaner than I had imagined, with a finely shaped head and silvery hair. "Distinguished" was a word one could use to describe him, but it was more than that. Shallow people can look distinguished. Hartleigh looked like a man who had suffered. At this unguarded moment while he gazed at the setting sun the lines of pain were marked deep and clear in his delicate features, and I was almost certain now that the gossip I had heard was false. My second picture of him had been closer to the truth. The

gentle, worn face, the slender hands lying half-open on his
knees, his expression of sadness – all belonged to a man who
cared no longer about carnal things, a man who was resigned
to sorrow. A book lay on the table beside him – a book and a
glass of water. His tweed jacket was stained and shabby, but
his white silk shirt was immaculately clean. My second picture had been amazingly accurate, I thought.

As I stepped toward him, he looked up and saw me.

"Good evening, sir," I said. "My name's David Brent, and
I've come out from England to see you."

"That's very charming of you," he said in a voice that was
surprisingly young and clear. "But are you sure you've come
to the right place? My name's Norman Hartleigh."

"I know."

"I never imagined that anyone would come out from England to see me at my time of life. You're not a tax collector, I
trust?"

I shook my head.

"Nor a detective? Good. Now, first let me get you a drink
and then you can tell me just what you really are. What
would you like? I'm drinking gin, but there's whisky if you
prefer it."

"Whisky would be fine," I said, wondering if the gin in his
glass was neat.

"Luku!" he shouted, clapping his hands. "Lete whisky na
soda na bilari."

Then he turned to me and smiled ruefully.

"I'm afraid there's no ice," he said. "We have to do without
some of the creature comforts of life out here. I never put ice
in whisky. But oh, how I do miss it in a dry Martini!"

Evidently he was not quite as ascetic as I had supposed.

"I don't miss the daily papers a bit," he continued. "They
never contain anything *really* interesting. The Sunday papers
are different. I have them sent out to me. The Sunday *Times*,
the *Observer*, and the *News of the World*, of course. What vitality, what *material!* Are you a journalist? No. Don't tell me until
your drink is beside you. Luku!" he shouted.

The tall thin boy appeared with a bottle of Black Label and a siphon on a tray. I glanced at the book on the table. It was by Simenon.

"Please help yourself," Hartleigh said, and carried on a running commentary while I poured out my drink.

"You must take more than that. There's not a drop more where it comes from. I say that to encourage you, because if you don't drink it, others – and I name no names – will. After coming out all the way from England you must need a drink. Don't you hate people who have those nasty little silver measures? As if our needs could be measured with a thimble. Sit down and take a swig. That's right. Now, perhaps you'll tell me what you've come to see me about."

The moment had come, and I could not find the right words to use. I dreaded having to mention the name Daphne Moore. Hartleigh was obviously a very different person from the young diplomat who had been in love with her, and I had been wrong about the glass of water. But the lines of suffering were real enough. His poise and flippancy were superficial. Whatever I said was bound to reopen the wound.

"Don't hurry yourself," Hartleigh murmured. "There's plenty of time. All evening, in fact."

I decided to plunge straight in.

"I've come to see you because the company I work for wants to make a film of the life of Daphne Moore," I said.

There was silence. I forced myself to look at Hartleigh. His eyes were fixed on the darkening plain. His face was expressionless. Then he spoke.

"That old bitch," he said.

I stared at him in amazement. He turned toward me.

"I suppose you work for that wretched film company that has been pestering me for the last two months? I might have guessed it. Well, I can tell you this. They can write to me, they can send cables, they can send bright young men out from England till they're blue in the face. But they'll never get a word of permission out of me to make that film so long as I live."

His hands were trembling with rage.

"I'm sorry to have made you angry," I said. "I only want to say that I thought . . ."

"Never mind what you thought," he interrupted. "I can guess what you thought from the stupid, vulgar letters I was sent. You supposed I would be flattered to be made the sentimental hero in your cheap little film. You supposed I would be pleased that every dolt in the world with sixpence in his pocket should think I was the lover of that meretricious, flabby old woman. Well, you were wrong, as you can see. You were wrong."

I picked up my glass and put it down on the tray. It was still half full. I stood up.

Hartleigh did not even look at me. He was calmer now, but he was still breathing heavily.

"Sit down and finish your drink. I've got nothing against you personally. Some people have to work in the sewers."

"It's kind of you to put it with such charm," I said coldly.

At that moment, from out of the dusk, a farm truck came clattering down the track. It was moving fast. For an instant I thought it would hit the corner of the house, but it swerved just in time and drew up in a cloud of dust outside the veranda opposite Hartleigh's chair. As it stopped, a young man sprang out of the driver's seat, leaped onto the veranda, and stood there smiling at us. He was wearing a khaki shirt and slacks. A light blue scarf was tied loosely around his neck. On his head was a wide-brimmed planter's hat which he now took off. He needed a haircut badly. His straw-colored hair was matted in curls. He was of medium height with powerful shoulders and a narrow waist. He was built like a tough, but his gentle blue eyes and the delicate nostrils of his small fleshy nose together with his wide nervous mouth, made him look sensitive.

"I might have known that as soon as I turned my back you'd open the Black Label," he said, laughing. Then an anxious look came into his eyes, and the smile left his face.

"Have I done anything wrong?" he asked. "Am I in the dog

house? Why don't you say 'hullo' and introduce me to your friend?"

"Bill, you must help me," Hartleigh said. "This is David Brent, who has come all the way from England to see me, and I've lost my temper and made him very angry and I'm afraid he wants to go."

Bill looked at me for a second and then picked up my half-empty glass.

"Whatever Norman's done you mustn't leave without finishing your drink," he said, handing it to me. "Please don't go. We only get visitors once in a blue moon, and Norman gets bored stiff just hearing me nattering away all day long. Come on," he said, putting a heavy arm around my shoulder. "Sink that down and let's move inside. Norman will catch his death of cold if he stays outside much longer. Come on! Sink it down. After all, I haven't done anything to offend you."

"Not as yet," Hartleigh murmured, smiling at me without a trace of shame.

Even when my vanity is hurt I can never be cross for long. I allowed myself to be propelled by Bill into the house. After all, I thought, I must at least make one more attempt to persuade Hartleigh to give us permission. My best chance of success was to get to know him.

As we walked into the living room, another picture slid into my mind. Perhaps Hartleigh was slightly deranged and Bill was the warder who coped with him when the moon was full. That would explain a lot of things. But now that his fit of rage was over, Hartleigh seemed perfectly sane. He was asking me questions about books and plays in England while Bill poured us out drinks. His questions were not designed to pass away the time; he was honestly eager to hear the answers.

When we settled down with our drinks I looked around at the room. It was about twenty feet long and a dozen feet wide. Only the fireplace and the floor were in brick. The walls were of dried mud, whitewashed over, and in places the damp had left ugly smears. In one corner, moisture from the thatched roof had run down in gray streaks. The thick beams supporting the thatch and the stained walls reminded me of a derelict Sussex cottage. But the room was quite well-furnished. There was nothing elaborate or fussy. The fawn-colored armchairs and the plain oak table, the light chintz curtains and rush matting on the floor were pleasant to look at. A landscape by Nevinson hung over the fireplace. The light came from two pressure lamps which hissed at each other from opposite ends of the room.

Hartleigh was now asking me about a recent exhibition of modern painting at the Leicester Galleries, and I was answering as best I could. He was thirsty for information about books and paintings – never about people. I wondered whether Bill felt left out of the conversation. I looked at him. Bill was sprawling in an armchair by the fire with his long legs stretched out in front of him. There was a smile trembling around his broad mouth as he watched Hartleigh, and a look of startling tenderness in his eyes.

"Did you have a good day?" Hartleigh asked him suddenly.

"Not so bad," Bill said. "I got thirty pounds for the four cows."

"How much did we pay for them?"

"Twenty-five."

"At least it's a profit."

"It can buy us another two bottles of whisky."

"Was there anyone amusing at the market?"

I thought I detected a note of deliberate casualness in Hartleigh's voice.

"Just the usual crowd," Bill said. The blue eyes were half-closed, defensively.

"Can't we persuade you to stay to dinner?" Hartleigh asked, turning toward me.

"That's a great idea," Bill cried. "We can open a bottle of wine."

"Thanks, but I'm afraid I can't," I said, glancing at my watch. "I'm dining with the Leytons, and I'm late as it is."

"So you're the man who's – who's staying with Ma Bolting," Bill said, and blushed.

He had been about to say "who's dining there." He had seen the danger in time, but he had swerved away too clumsily. For an instant Hartleigh's eyes flickered toward him. He had noticed.

"You're not late," Hartleigh said to me. "They never sit down to dinner before nine o'clock, so I'm told."

I finished my drink and stood up.

"I shall have to go slow because I don't know the roads," I explained.

"I hope you'll dine with us another night."

"I've got an idea," Bill said. "Why don't you ask him to dine on Thursday? I've got to drive across to Iringa that day so you'll be able to natter away together without me butting in."

Hartleigh turned toward Bill and looked at him as if he were seeing an acquaintance he had known long ago.

"I hope our guest will dine here on Thursday," he said. "But surely you can get back from Iringa in time?"

"I've a mass of chores to do. I have to get a haircut for a start."

"That won't take all day."

Bill was standing awkwardly with his weight on one foot, stroking the seams of his trousers with large red hands.

"Sometimes one has to wait for hours," he said. "Besides, I've got a lot of farm stuff to buy."

There was silence. Two enormously fat bugs were circling around the pressure lamp on the desk, battering alternately against the glass. Bill caught one of them in each hand and threw them into the fire.

"As a matter of fact, I thought of staying the night in Iringa," he muttered. "I don't like driving back late at night in the dark."

"We'll talk about it later," Hartleigh said quietly. "Mr. Brent now wants to go."

Bill picked up a flashlight from the table.

"It's dark outside. I'll see you to your car," he said.

Hartleigh walked across the room and opened the door.

"Can you dine here on Thursday?" he asked.

"I'd love to. Thanks very much. Good night."

"Come at seven if you can. I've some good sherry," he called after me.

The air was crisp and cold. I was glad I had a sweater in the back of the car. Bill and I walked up the track in silence. I was trying to think of something to say when he spoke.

"Can I call you David?" he asked.

"Heavens, yes," I said.

"After all, you're not much older than me."

"Only old enough to be your father."

"Rot. What's your age?"

"Forty."

"I'm twenty-six. You'd have had to start pretty young."

"That's just what I did," I said.

He laughed, but I could feel that for some reason he was still nervous.

"I know you're a type I can trust," he suddenly blurted out of the darkness. "I just know."

"Why do you?"

"Because of your face, for a start."

"I wouldn't trust a man with a face like mine farther than I could spit," I said.

"You'd be wrong, wouldn't you?"

We had reached my car. He switched off the flashlight. Neither of us moved.

"What's the secret?" I asked.

"How do you know there's a secret?"

"When a man tells you he trusts you, it generally means he's longing to tell you something in confidence."

"You've almost hit the nail on the head. Almost, but not quite. There's something I want you to *do* for me in confidence. Is it awful nerve my asking you?"

"That depends on what you want me to do."

"It's only to give someone a message, but in confidence,

mind you. Not letting anyone else know what the message is."

"I expect I can do that," I said, "if I meet the person."

My eyes were now used to the darkness. I could see his hands moving nervously. I wondered what was coming. I have noticed that complete strangers will reveal to one the secrets they would never dream of telling their friends. For some reason they feel safer with an outsider than a member of their own circle. Perhaps they think that a stranger has less temptation to be indiscreet, or perhaps they take an optimistic view of human nature.

"You may not get the chance," Bill said. "But if you're alone for a moment with Mary Leyton could you tell her that I'll definitely be in Iringa on Thursday? Could you?"

I felt slightly disappointed. I had expected a more dramatic message.

"I could," I said. "And I will."

"Thanks. Thanks ever so much."

He grasped my hand and held it as if I had promised him a fortune. I got into my car and switched on the light by the dashboard. He peered in at me. He was worried again.

"It's in confidence, isn't it?" he asked anxiously. "I mean, you won't tell Norman, will you?"

"No," I said, and started the engine.

But he was still worried.

"It's not for the reason you might think," he said in a voice husky with embarrassment. "Norman's really fond of Mary. They get on fine together. But he's afraid there'll be trouble."

"He may well be right."

"Never."

"You're a fool, Bill," I said. "But God bless you."

"Can I call in at Ma Bolting's tomorrow after dark?"

"If you want to."

"There might be news, mightn't there?"

"That's true," I said. "There might. Good night, Bill."

"Good night. And thanks a million," he shouted as the car moved away.

# 5

Driving at night in the Southern Highlands is a good time for reflection. The roads are so pitted you cannot drive fast, and the country is so open you can see the headlights of a car a mile away. As I drove toward the Leytons' property I wondered whether I had any hope of persuading Norman Hartleigh to change his mind about the film. Evidently he was not rich. When I got to know him better I must at least tell him of Stonor's offer. Perhaps young Bill could help me. I wondered about Norman Hartleigh and young Bill. I decided that I had been wrong to form any coherent picture of their lives before meeting them. I had tried to reach the truth too quickly. I must now discard all romantic notions of Hartleigh and examine the plain facts, selecting them and placing them in their proper place like a jigsaw puzzle.

But the facts would not fit together. Bill was in love with Mary Leyton, and Hartleigh disapproved because he was afraid Barry Leyton would find out and make trouble. That much was clear. Hartleigh was not jealous, and Bill was fond of him. All right. But why had Hartleigh been so furious when I mentioned Daphne Moore's name? Why did he now dislike her so bitterly? He had once loved her. The facts were there to prove it: I had checked them carefully before I started to write my treatment. The facts supported the very story I had told at the film conference. I had taken one slight liberty with the time sequence. In reality, the farewell meeting between Hartleigh and Daphne Moore had taken place a fortnight after the last performance of the play, in July, 1928. Their affair had lasted until that moment. In the film, I had decided that it was more dramatic for their farewell scene to occur immediately after the emotional excitement of the first night party. That was the only inaccuracy in my treatment. I was certain of it.

I slowed down. There were two little green lamps ahead of me. Then I saw that they belonged to an enormous brown owl in the middle of the road. It was peering into the headlights without moving. I sounded my horn. The owl took no notice. Ten yards away I stopped and switched off the car lights and walked toward it. Awkwardly, yet without any haste, the owl spread its jagged wings and flew slowly away.

I was glad I had stopped. A short distance ahead two white posts marked the turning where a track ran off the road into a glade of trees. I knew from Mrs. Bolting's map that this track led to the Leytons' house. As I got back into my car I tried to remember what Tim and Mrs. Bolting had told me about the Leytons. It was not much. I knew that Barry Leyton was twenty years older than his wife and had a fierce temper; I knew that their only child had died of typhoid four years previously, and that Mary Leyton was liked by almost everyone in the district.

For a mile I drove through the macrocarpa trees. Then, dramatically, the avenue opened out into a wide expanse of gravel flanked by a stone balustrade. As I drove up, a dozen lamps supported by wrought-iron figures on the balustrade were switched on so that the whole façade of the house was suddenly illuminated. I got out of the car and gazed up in amazement. Four huge white pillars ran up the three stories of the house and joined a vast pediment. The façade reminded me of a set we had once built for "Vanity Fair." It had looked fantastic enough in the studio; here, in the wilds of Africa, it was wholly unreal.

An African boy in white trousers and a white coat cut like an Eton jacket came tripping down the steps toward me.

"Jambo, Bwana," he said. "This way please. This way."

He led me into a hall full of sporting prints and pointed to a door on the left. I forced my face into the idiotic expression one assumes when meeting strangers and turned the handle and walked forward radiating human kindness mixed with appropriate diffidence. But my efforts were wasted. He had shown me into a washroom with rows of lotions on glass

shelves and shining green tiles. There were expensive towels
by the washbasin. I decided that if they wanted me to wash
then I would wash. I locked the door behind me, took off my
coat, and washed my face and hands in pleasantly hot water.
Scottish Heather seemed a more suitable lotion for me to use
than Milles Fleurs, but it was stronger than I had thought.
Redolent of moorland, I walked back into the hall where the
boy was still waiting. This time he led me to the end of the
hall. Standing by an oak door was another boy who looked
about twelve. He was wearing a khaki shirt and shorts. As I
approached I was amazed by the look of fear in his eyes. With
an effort he turned the handle of the heavy door. Once again
I composed my features and walked into a long drawing
room decorated in the off-white style that was fashionable for
a while in London long before the war.

From the far end of the brightly lit room a young woman
came forward to greet me. She was wearing a dark green
satin dress. Mrs. Bolting had told me that Mary Leyton was
twenty-eight, but she looked younger. She was very attractive. Yet it was hard to explain why. Though she had a lovely
figure, her neck seemed too fragile to support her head. Her
nose was too short and her lips were too thin and curling.
But the contrast between the heavy chestnut-brown hair and
violet eyes was entrancing. The skin beneath her eyes was
unlined and a little fleshy, which gave her an innocent look.
When she smiled one small crease appeared beneath each
eye. Perhaps therein lay the charm.

"You've arrived!" she said, smiling up at me as if I were a
knight come to rescue her. "You got here all alone. It's brilliant of you. Barry's out in the pantry teaching Rosti to make
a dry Martini. But I've made us two pink gins on the sly.
Would you like one?"

She led me over to a lacquer table bristling with bottles.

"Shall I tell you something in confidence?" she asked,
gazing up at me with a sudden change to seriousness as she
handed me the drink. "Do you promise on your word of
honor never to tell anyone?"

Here it comes again, I thought as I nodded my head. Her wide eyes stared at me solemnly.

"Well, it's this," she said in a loud stage whisper. "I don't believe that Rosti will *ever* learn to make a dry Martini.

"Mark you, I intend no slur on the African race as a whole," she murmured as we moved across to a large ivory-colored sofa by the fire, "but something tells me this boy Rosti is not quite as bright as others are. Not that I would ever dream of revealing the fact – even to Barry's most reactionary friends, who like to believe all Africans are dotty."

"How did this place come to be planted in the middle of Africa?" I asked, waving my arm around the room.

"Ages back – at least twenty years ago – Barry burned the bricks, and planted the trees, and brought out an architect from London. Then, ten years ago, I was brought out, and he planted me."

"I'm still bewildered. How do you get electric light?"

"Engines and things. You must ask Barry. He loves explaining all about it. But I want to hear all the London gossip."

While we talked I tried to find an opportunity to give her Bill's message in a casual way as if it had no importance. Though I was quite interested in the affair because it might give me the idea for a film story, I did not want to be involved. I began to regret that I had allowed myself to be persuaded by Bill's eagerness. Then Mary Leyton gave me a chance.

"You've made a hit with Ma Bolting," she said.

"That reminds me. I forgot to give you a message," I began.

"Ma Bolting's the only institution we've got out here apart from the Christmas Eve dance," she said, interrupting me quickly. I looked at her in surprise. Then I saw that her eyes were fixed beyond me, across the room. I turned around. A man was standing in the doorway watching us. He was very lean, but so well proportioned that it was not until he moved toward us that I realized he was small. He was wearing a checked suit and a white polo sweater. He walked with a slight limp. He was about fifty.

"Good evening," he said, shaking my hand. "I'm sorry there are no other guests to greet you. We asked the Cobbs over, but their child is ill so they can't come. Cocktails will be here in a minute."

"We were talking about Ma Bolting," Mary Leyton murmured.

"She's a fine old girl, but I should think her place is pretty poky to stay in."

"I'm comfortable enough," I said.

He stared at me for a moment and then walked over to the chimney piece and moved a T'ang horse two inches to the left.

"One day I shall build a really decent hotel in these parts," he announced.

"And who will come and stay in it?" his wife asked, playing with the gold tassel of a sofa cushion.

"Plenty of people," he answered defiantly. "We'd get the very best people out here if it was comfortable enough."

"Then let's thank Providence for our discomforts," she said.

In the silence that followed a tall houseboy came in, carrying a tray. He was wearing the same white uniform as the boy who had showed me in, and his large hands were covered by white cotton gloves so that the only black part of him that showed was his head. On the tray was a large silver cocktail shaker. The three glasses grouped around it were also made of silver, and I was afraid they would taste of metal polish. The boy's hands shook a little as he handed a glass to each of us in turn.

"Cover them up in clothes from head to foot and they smell less," Barry Leyton said as the boy left the room.

"But I'm told we smell horrible to them," his wife said. "So nauseating they nearly faint."

"What's that got to do with it? Let's sink these down and go into dinner. I've been out all day on the farm, and I'm simply ravenous."

"Perhaps Mr. Brent would like another glass?"

I gulped down the drink. There was no taste of polish, but there was too much vermouth.

"No, thanks," I said.

Mary Leyton stretched out her arms and rose from the sofa as if she were waking from a dream, and we walked in to dinner.

6

The dining-room furniture had obviously been brought out from England. Two late Georgian candelabras gleamed on a polished table flanked by chairs of the same period. Set into the walls, which were paneled in dark oak, portraits, presumably of the Leyton family, glared down at us through layers of yellow varnish. The food was simple and well-cooked, and Barry Leyton surprised me by being an almost over-attentive host. As Corton followed Montrachet my glass was constantly refilled so that I began to feel pleasantly relaxed. Only the faces of the two houseboys who waited at table could remind us that thousands of miles of Africa lay spread around outside.

"When I first came out here," Barry Leyton was saying, "I couldn't get the hang of their Swahili names at all. It's an idiotic language anyhow, with Arabic and English names all mixed up. *Bafu* for bath, *sokisi* for socks. Just ridiculous. So I called my first boy Supu and my second Rosti and my third boy Deserti and so on. We've got a Fruti in the kitchen now and a *toto*, that's a little boy, called Nuti, who looks after the fires. They don't mind. In fact, it rather amuses them."

"Rosti's the expert on dry Martinis," Mary Leyton said, winking at the ceiling.

"She's teasing me, as usual, but she's hopeless at dealing with them. I don't know where she'd be without me."

"Where indeed?" Mary asked the ceiling. Then suddenly she smiled at him, and I saw from the light in her eyes that for all the tension that seemed to exist between them some trace of affection still remained.

While Barry told me of his efforts to build and maintain the property I examined him more closely. His staring brown eyes and slightly hooked nose jutting out over a short upper lip gave him an arrogant look. His lips were thick and sensual. Though he was small he gave the impression of being immensely strong. One felt that beneath his loosely fitting clothes lay muscles that were taut and overdeveloped. The skin of his face was red and shiny, and in places threads of blue veins showed through the hard surface. He was almost ugly, yet when he glowed with excitement as he talked about his property he exuded a strong, rather animal charm. It was easy to see that he was attractive to women.

By now I had learned a little of his past. He had been the only son of rich parents who had fondly allowed him to pursue his ambition to become one of the best racing drivers in England. In this he had succeeded. Then, when he was lying third on the last lap in a race at Brooklands, his car had crashed. A month later he was told by a specialist that a nerve in his leg had been damaged. Though he would be able to drive a car, it was unlikely that he would be able to race again. His other interest had been farming. Six months later he went out to Tanganyika and bought the ground which now surrounded us. He had met Mary on a brief visit to England a year before the war. I wondered what they had in common.

Mary's father, I had gathered by now, was a landowner in Norfolk. Mary had come down from London for a weekend to rest from her activities as a gay debutante. Barry had been staying at a house in the neighborhood, and they had met by chance. Why had she married a man twenty years older than herself?

I watched her as she sat making a pattern with almonds on the table while her husband talked about the diesel engine and dynamo that supplied the house with electricity. Her nails were cut short and unvarnished, which made her fingers look blunt, yet they moved delicately, caressing each almond they touched, as if each finger had a life of its own. While I watched her furtively, she lifted a finger to her mouth and touched it with the tip of her tongue. Then, as I looked at her mouth, the corners drawn upward, the curling lips a little parted, I suddenly realized what she and her husband had in common. They were both sensual. They were animals of different breeds, but they were male and female and they lusted for each other.

At that moment, probably because I was tired and had drunk too much, an uninvited picture flashed into my mind, and I saw them as they were alone together, with all pretense stripped away. Mary's arms were folded behind her head, and she was gazing up at his sinewy red body. And as he bent down toward her she gave a little shiver.

I must have frowned, because Mary turned toward me inquiringly.

"Six cylinders is quite enough," Barry was saying.

"More than enough, I would think," Mary said with sudden enthusiasm.

"You don't know anything about it."

"Nor I do. But I'm longing for coffee, and it's time we made our guest talk about himself."

"Tim Curry says you've come out here to find a story for the films," Barry said as the boy called Rosti poured out coffee.

"That's right."

"I should have thought you could find better material in Nairobi."

"Nairobi's been done," I replied truthfully.

"I don't know what you'll find of interest in these parts."

"Susan Curry," Mary said. "She's madly interesting."

"Susan Curry's a perfectly good woman," Barry began.

"That's just it. That goodness and those teeth. On the screen I would have thought that the combination would be irresistible."

"We're all pretty normal ordinary people up here," Barry said, frowning at her.

"As normal as the day is long," she murmured.

"There's only one odd chap in the neighborhood," he continued. "And I advise you to have nothing to do with him."

"Who's that?" I asked innocently.

"A man called Norman Hartleigh."

"I think Norman's a pet," Mary said.

"We don't want that sort up here."

"What sort?"

"You know perfectly well," he said, glowering at her. "The District Officer's got an eye on him already. Let's move. The room's getting stuffy."

The drawing room was full of smoke from the log fire. For a moment we stood in silence by the sofa with our eyes watering.

"Let's open all the windows," Mary said. "It's quite warm outside."

While I began opening the long French windows that led out into the garden Barry strode across to the fireplace and began poking at the fire vigorously.

"I've told that boy time and time again that if this fire's not kept up it smokes," he said. As he turned toward her I saw that his mouth was twisted in rage.

"Perhaps he didn't understand you," Mary said. For the first time the teasing lilt had left her voice.

"You know perfectly well he understood me."

"Then perhaps he forgot. He's only a toto. Children of twelve do forget things. They're made that way."

"He won't forget again in a hurry."

"Barry, what does it matter? We don't need a fire, anyhow."

"I like to see a fire burning in November."

"But we're not in England."

"I want this fire burning. And I don't like this room full of smoke. And it won't be full of smoke tomorrow night."

"Darling, let me talk to him in the morning. I'm sure Nuti won't forget again."

Nuti was obviously the little boy who had opened the door for me.

"He won't forget again," Mary repeated.

"I'm sure he won't," Barry said softly. "Excuse me."

He went over to a desk behind the sofa and took out a leather whip and walked quickly out of the room.

"Don't . . ." Mary began, and then stopped.

As the door closed behind him she walked over to the drink tray. "Will you have a liqueur?" she asked in a brittle voice.

"No, thanks," I said.

I was still staring at the door. For once I was shocked. Mary came over to me and touched my arm.

"Listen to me," she said. "It's not as bad as you think. Other people fine them from their wages, and that's mean because totos only get eight shillings a month. Like this it's quickly finished and done with."

"It doesn't look pretty either way."

"That's what I thought when I first came out here. I made up my mind I'd never see them punished in any way. I'd be gentle and kind to all of them. But when they're deliberately stupid and lazy they get on my nerves and I nag at them. The plain result is they respect Barry and they despise me. That's the way it is with them. Stay out here some time and you'll understand what I'm trying to say."

She wandered across to the lacquer table and poured out a glass of water.

"I like Ma Bolting, don't you?" she asked suddenly.

As she spoke I remembered the message.

"She's a honey," I said. "By the way, I forgot to give you a message. It's not a bit important. It was only to say that Bill Wayne's going over to Iringa on Thursday."

"You saw him tonight?"

"Yes. I had drinks with Norman Hartleigh before I came here."

"And Bill gave you that message?"

"That's right."

She gazed at me in silence for a while. I thought that she was trying to guess what I was thinking, and I made my face blank.

"You did that very well," she said, after a pause.

"What do you mean?"

"The vagueness, the light tone of voice, the timing. Nearly perfect. Perhaps a shade forced."

"I still don't understand."

"Yes you do. Not everything. But quite a bit. And it doesn't matter. See? Bill has an instinct about people. I suspect he was right to trust you. Thank you for giving me the message, and thank you for being so tactful about it."

As she spoke I realized that she could have no idea how much Bill had told me.

"I should have thought it was a mistake to trust a stranger," I said.

Perhaps she smiled at me because I sounded pompous.

"So should I," she said. "And you're such a *complete* stranger. You're a stranger all over – from top to toe. Will you be seeing Bill tomorrow?"

"I think so."

"Will you tell him that I have to be in Iringa on Thursday? Shopping. I have to buy an elephant or two and a bottle of angostura."

At that moment she looked so young that I felt I must try to be old and sensible.

"Are you being wise?" I asked.

"No."

"Doesn't disaster lie ahead?"

"I don't think so," she said. "You see, just supposing any-one did dare to tell the person most concerned, he'd never believe it. And there'll never be any proof. Never."

"How can you be sure?"

"Because Africa's a large place. Far too large for my liking. I feel like a pin on a billiard table."

Her tone of voice had changed. I turned around. Barry was standing in the doorway. Either she had acute hearing or she knew by instinct when he was coming.

Barry threw the whip into a corner.

"What about a drink for our guest?" he asked jovially.

"No, thanks," I said.

He walked over to Mary and put a hand on her shoulder. "Don't you think I've got a lovely wife?" he asked.

When he had left the room his voice had shown no trace of drink. It was now thick and slurred. But he had only been away for a few minutes.

"Don't you think she's lovely?" he repeated.

"Lovely," I said.

For a moment there was silence. Far away in the valley a hyena was crying to the moon, the howl rising in menace, then falling in a moan of anguish.

"Stay for another drink," Barry ordered. His fingers began to stroke the nape of Mary's neck.

"It's late," I said. "I must go."

As I moved toward them to say good-bye his fingers were moving up and down her neck with slow rhythmic strokes. Suddenly Mary gave a little shiver.

"Just one for the road," Barry said.

His eyes were shining and he was breathing heavily.

I thanked them and said good-bye quickly. There was still a lot of smoke in the room, and I felt rather sick.

## 7

The next morning I woke up late and found a cable lying on the table beside my bed. Presumably Shabete had brought it in while I was asleep. It was from Stonor, in his usual style. I could see him dictating it impatiently to a secretary. Making allowances for various errors in spelling which had crept in during its relay through Africa, which had taken three days, I found that Stonor had cabled:

WHAT NEWS HARTLEIGH QUERY GO ON SAFARI THEN AIRMAIL QUICKLIEST POSSIBLE SYNOPSIS AFRICAN LOVE STORY SUITABLE FOR JUDY GRANT AND DICK CALPE MAKING FULL USE LOCAL BACKGROUND WAR DANCES ETCETERA STOP GREAT INTEREST HERE FROM WIDMORE PICTURES POSSIBLE COMBINE STONOR

Over a beer in the bar I wrote out a reply on the cable form that Mrs. Bolting had given me:

HARTLEIGH REFUSES PERMISSION BUT AM STILL TRYING STOP NOT MAN TO BE HURRIED STOP GOING ON SAFARI SHORTLY WILL BE OUT OF TOUCH THREE WEEKS BRENT

When I reread the cable I saw that Stonor might think that *I* was the man who was not to be hurried. Nothing was more calculated to enrage him. I therefore inserted the word "Hartleigh" in between "stop" and "not" and handed the cable to Mrs. Bolting who gave it to Shabete to give to the native bus driver when he passed the following day.

"I hope he doesn't forget," she said.

"Which one?" I asked. "Shabete or the bus driver?"

"Either of them," she replied placidly.

Evidently communication between the Rest House and the outer world was a matter of chance.

That afternoon I took my notebook and walked across the dry bristling scrub toward the hill at the back of the house. It was a bright afternoon, and the wide blue sky seemed very far away. When I reached the crest of the hill I had the impression I was standing on the highest peak in the world. I felt dazed yet exhilarated. I sat down on a boulder and tried to think of a film story while I stared down at the scorched plain below. No original story lit up my mind, so I wrote down some of the anecdotes Mrs. Bolting had told me and tried not to think about Wanda.

About an hour later I heard the sound of a bell. It could only be the ship's bell on the terrace of the Rest House. I wondered why it was being rung so violently. Then, as if in reply, the drums started to beat in the valley. I looked around and noticed a thin red streak on the horizon to the south. At first I could not believe it was a fire. I could see no smoke, and the red streak seemed motionless. Then as I stood up I saw that it was slowly twisting and curling and moving closer. The wind was blowing from the south toward the Rest House. I picked up my notebook and walked down the hill. I could now see the long row of little flames advancing like a division in line. One section would be partly held up by a thicket or a damp piece of ground so that it almost seemed to withdraw. Then it would surge forward again into position, and the line would advance relentlessly. I began to run.

From every direction boys were running toward the Rest House. I found Mrs. Bolting on the terrace directing operations like a general. Beside her were stacks of leafy branches to use as fire brooms. As I arrived a truck crammed with black bodies drew up, and about twenty boys swarmed out, already carrying branches, and rushed toward her. She turned quickly to me.

"Take these boys to the southwest firebreak," she said, thrusting a branch into my hand. "We're going to try to hold the fire there."

"Where is it?"

"There," she cried, pointing. "Where did you think it was? North?"

She shouted something in Swahili and the boys moved toward me.

"You'll find Bill there with his lot. Their property's safe so far," she bellowed after me as we began to run down the hill. "Free drinks on the house tonight if it's still standing."

I could now hear the roar of the fire as it rushed across the dry scrub, crackling as it devoured the grass and short bushes. Then we turned past a thicket, and I saw the line of flames close ahead, coiling and leaping with angry puffs, driving the buck and grasshoppers and locusts before it. Rows of boys were facing the line, crashing down their branches on the flames that spurted from the ground.

Bill gave a shout of welcome when he saw me and then gave quick orders in Swahili to the boys I had brought. His shirt was wet with sweat, and there were smudges of soot on his face. His teeth looked very white when he grinned at me.

"Where's the firebreak?" I asked. I was still panting for breath.

"The fire leaped over it half an hour ago. Our only chance now is to attack it from either end and hold it at the last firebreak before the house. You came just in time."

For the next few hours I was in a daze of heat and fatigue, but I can remember Ma Bolting's wild war whoop when she charged in to join our forces with a towel tied around her head. It made her look far more barbaric than the half-naked Africans. With her she brought yet more squads of boys who had come from properties far outside the district, sent across by farmers she had never met. They came without any message. The fire was a common danger. No explanation was needed.

With darkness the fire seemed more menacing. And still we crashed down our leafy branches on the flames, beating until the leaves were burned, and with aching arms we must cut more branches, beating steadily, stamping out the tongues that leaped across the last firebreak, choking and gasping as our arms rose and fell, until, perhaps only two hours after sunset, the wind dropped, and the last flame was killed, and the ashes drifted slowly in the cold still air.

We were joined in the bar by Tim Curry who had driven over with a truckload of boys to fight the fire on the southeast side. Grime ran in streaks down his broad face, and his hair lay flat on his head like a cap.

"Jay Cobb and Barry Leyton would have driven over to help," he said, "but they've had a fire near the club. It's under control now."

"The boys say the rains will come tomorrow," Ma Bolting said. "Have a double whisky."

After we had had three rounds on the house I suggested it was time I paid for some drinks.

"Whose fire was it? Mine or yours?" she asked.

Tim Curry looked at his watch.

"I must get cracking or I'll get the stick from the wife,"

he said. He moved in his shy, awkward way toward the door. Then he turned to me.

"The wife hopes you'll come over for drinks toward sundown tomorrow evening," he said.

"I'd love to."

"Thanks for the drinks, Ma."

"Thanks for putting out my fire."

"Good night, all."

He left the room quickly. Ma Bolting looked at Bill, who was sprawling in a corner.

"One more drink and then off you go, young man," she said. "You'll catch a bad chill lying about in those sweaty clothes."

Bill did not move.

"What about a spot of grub?" he asked, winking at me.

"The impudence of the boy! As if he'd got no food at home!" she said, winking at me in her turn.

"Not a sausage," he said happily. "The boys will have gone to bed ages ago."

"Won't your . . . won't Mr. Hartleigh be waiting up for you?"

When she stumbled in mid-sentence I knew that she suspected and disapproved. Her face was now glowing with embarrassment. Bill seemed unaware of the awkward pause.

"Course he won't," he said. "He'll be fast asleep by now."

Ma Bolting looked at him in silence. Though her face was grim, I could see that she was fond of him.

"Very well, then," she said, recovering her boisterous spirits. "But not one bite until you've had a shower and a rubdown. David had better lend you a shirt and sweater. I'll tell the boys to have food ready in half an hour. Now, off you go, the two of you."


Bill insisted that I take the first shower while the water was still hot. When he came back from the bathroom next door I was half-dressed. He took a cigarette from his trousers, which were hanging on a chair, and I threw him a box of matches.

He stood naked in front of the fire drying himself, and suddenly I felt old and very tired.

"What are you looking so sad about?" Bill asked, squatting down on his haunches.

"I was thinking that I was positively middle-aged."

"You didn't do all that badly today."

"But I shall be a wreck tomorrow."

I threw him a clean shirt. "You'd better get dressed," I said.

He did not move. He was watching me with anxious blue eyes.

"Any news?" he asked awkwardly.

"Yes. Mary Leyton will be in Iringa on Thursday."

"And that's tomorrow," he said slowly in an awed voice. "This time tomorrow we'll be together."

He sprang up and stretched out his arms exultantly. "God, life can be good!" he said.

His eyes were shining with happiness. What use would it have been if I had tried to warn him? He would never have listened to me.

"Don't forget that Norman's expecting you at seven-thirty," he said, as he began to dress.

"I'm looking forward to it."

"You won't . . ."

"No," I said, interrupting him. "I won't. I promise you that."

"Thanks, David. Thanks a lot. One day I'll tell you the whole story and you'll see it's all right. But now . . ."

"But now," I said, "let's go and give Ma Bolting a pink gin before dinner."


I was tired and rather drunk when I went to bed that night. I could still hear the flames crackling over the scrub. Suddenly I realized that I had forgotten to register how the fire could be shot in Technicolor. I was slipping. Perhaps Africa was getting me.

## 8

I drove across to the Currys' house the following afternoon. The sky was gray, and thunder was growling in the distance. I could see flashes of lightning beyond the swamp. At last the rain was approaching. A small track crossed over a wide plain of scrub to the kind of house you would expect to find a retired colonel living in near Camberley. It was trimly built in red brick. A crazy pavement led up to a neat porch. As I arrived a brown dog rushed up to the car, barking wildly and scampering dangerously near the fender. Tim and Susan Curry came out to greet me.

Susan Curry was a small perky woman of about forty. She wore a low-cut tightly fitting green dress with a yellow belt. Her make-up looked as if it had been put on in a hurry. Her teeth were large – out of all proportion to her mouth – and very white. She was energetic and cheerful. Though I wanted to look around the farm, she hurried me into a brightly furnished living room, and the three of us sat down.

Tim was even shier than usual. His large red hands were folded on his lap and his face was sullen with embarrassment. He spoke little. But Susan Curry asked me polite questions about the film world, which I answered as best I could until I saw that she was longing to tell me about her world and her problems. She seized ravenously at the first question I asked her and was soon well away. I learned that their two children had been sent to bed early that night because they had been naughty. The native nurse spoiled them, and the houseboys were worse. Just wouldn't take any trouble. The boys in East Africa weren't worth their wages, however low. You had to be at them all the time. Then followed items of local news. The price of meat was rising, and Tim was trying to raise a stock of healthy native cattle. The District Officer had issued a warning that there was a shortage of maize in the area, and posho, made of maize, was the boys' staple diet. The mail truck had toppled into a ravine near Iringa. A lion had killed a native boy at Powaga. The rains were long overdue.

While she talked I gazed around at the crimson and green poufs on the floor, the fretwork shelves, probably made by Tim, over the mantelpiece, and the bright oleographs on the walls – a glen in Scotland complete with stag, a galleon in full sail, the coast of Cornwall, and three musketeers.

After a long half-hour Susan Curry paused and asked if I would like a drink.

"Beer or gin?" she asked.

"Gin, please," I said. By that time I would have drunk rubbing alcohol.

When we had settled down with our drinks, she asked me if I had enjoyed dinner with the Leytons.

"Hugely," I replied.

"I think that Barry Leyton is one of the finest types we've got in the whole of the Southern Highlands," she said. "He's friendly and helpful to nearly everyone. And he's got no swank about him. You'd never think he came from one of the greatest English families."

"Never," I said.

"I wish Mary wouldn't make those silly teasing remarks to him all the time. You can see they annoy him. And it isn't wise of her to put his back up. That young woman had better watch her step."

"How?" I asked.

"You must have heard the gossip. She's had her eye on Bill Wayne from the moment he came out here. I think it's disgusting – an older woman trying to lead on a mere youngster."

"She's only three years older," I said.

"I daresay. But she's married to a loyal husband. I still think it's disgusting."

"Susan, be fair," Tim murmured. "Nothing's known for certain."

"Why do you think Bill never comes here any more? I'll tell you why. Because she's jealous."

Susan Curry swung back to me. "When Tim goes off on safari I get quite lonely," she explained. "And Bill used to come up here two and three times a week for a gossip and a snack. It did him good to be in a healthy normal atmosphere, away from that man who's doing his best to ruin the boy's life."

"Ruin his life?"

"Tim tells me you've been over there. Haven't you seen how the man looks at the boy? It makes me sick."

"Now, Susan . . ." Tim began.

"I believe in telling the truth. That man's done his best to poison Bill's nature. I know his type. I can spot them a mile off. But he won't succeed with Bill, I can tell you that. Not in a month of Sundays."

While she spoke it began to rain. Susan went off to say good night to the children. Tim and I stood looking out of the broad window. The first heavy drops fell slowly and sparsely so that we could hear each patter on the ground. Then, as if a filter had been removed, the rain crashed down suddenly, beating onto the parched plain. And at once, thousands of flies and moths and beetles rose from the scrub in alarm, hovering uncertainly, falling with soaked wings, then rising again, drifting toward the shelter of the house, clustering around the porch, swarming in through a small opening in the far window, flapping against the glass of the kerosene lamps, flopping into the fire, while outside the rain poured down, churning up the earth, rushing in streams across the courtyard, gurgling out of the gutters below the house.

"At last," Tim said, closing the far window.

"And about time too," Susan added, as she came back into the room.

I looked at my watch. It was seven, and the road would now be slippery. I finished my drink. Then I turned toward Tim. Something Susan had said had given me an idea.

"Where do you go on safari?" I asked him.

"Round the native villages mostly, to buy cattle."

"Do you go alone?"

"I take a couple of boys with me."

"When do you next go off on safari?"

"In three days' time, as a matter of fact."

"How long will you be away?"

"A fortnight. I'll be back the week before Christmas. You wouldn't like to come with me, would you?"

"That's just what I've been fishing for."

"Fine!" he said, slapping his thigh. "Can you leave in three days' time?"

"Certainly."

"Well, that's splendid. I get bored stiff all by myself."

"Can you lay on a war dance?" I asked.

He grinned at me mischievously.

"With full war paint," he said.

"Now, don't tease the poor man," Susan protested.

"I can promise you to lay on some good shooting."

"What about primitive African life?"

"We'll be knee-deep in it," he said.

"Can I really come with you?"

"You can't get out of it now. You're a big game hunter already."

I thanked Tim warmly; I thanked them both for their hospitality. Tim lent me a mackintosh, and I drove off through the rain to dine with Norman Hartleigh.

## 9

The rain had turned the surface of the road into mud, and I had to drive in second gear all the way. I was late when my car slithered down the slope to Imunda. The tall boy, Luku, met me. He was wearing a ground sheet on his head, draped like a shawl. His long thin legs were smeared with mud. The rain was still falling steadily. A small pond had formed in the middle of the yard.

I found Norman Hartleigh in the living room swatting flies with a folded newspaper. He was wearing a blue suit that was shiny and frayed. His gray hair was brushed back over his scalp, and there was a pink flush about his face and hands as if he had just come out of a bath.

"With this rain Bill will probably stay the night in Iringa," he said, "so you'll have to put up with me all the evening alone. Will you take sherry?"

He walked over to a decanter on the side table and carefully filled the two glasses on the tray.

"No ice, no dry Martini," he said, handing me a glass with a slight bow.

At that stage of the evening his conversation and gestures were polite and restrained. I might have been drinking sherry with the senior tutor of my college. He was courteous but withdrawn. I felt that he was deliberately cheating me. After we had finished our drink he stood up.

"I believe we should go in to dinner," he said. "I don't want the cheese soufflé to be spoiled. I prepared it with my own fair hands."

He led the way into a small square room. Reproductions of some Leonardo da Vinci drawings hung on the whitewashed walls. Four candles burned on the narrow table. We sat down on high-backed wicker chairs, and Luku came in with the soufflé, which was deliciously soft and light.

"If there's no local product I always believe in drinking the wine of the nearest country," Hartleigh said as Luku poured out some hock. "This wine comes from Paarl. The burgundy we shall drink with our steak comes from Constantia."

He began a long discussion on wine. By the time he had reached Italy I was growing restive. If he intended to continue in this professorial strain I was in for a dull evening.

"You must excuse my conversation," he said suddenly, as if he had read my thoughts. "But, you see, I'm rusty. Bill and I know each other so well that we seldom talk. And when we do it's generally about farm affairs or the state of the weather and our stomachs. When I first knew Bill I tried to interest him in the things that interest me. It was hopeless. I had met him too late. His prejudices were already formed. And now, I wouldn't have it any different. I've spent half my life discussing art and literature with intelligent people. It's a relief to be with someone who seldom thinks. It's wonderfully restful."

He filled up my glass and then his own. Once again I noticed his long delicate hands. He looked up at me and smiled.

"When you came here the other day I'm afraid I was violently rude," he said. "I'm sorry. I think it was the shock of hearing that woman's name spoken aloud after so many years. You see, you didn't look like a film magnate."

"I'm not. I'm just a plain hack scriptwriter."

"I've never met a scriptwriter before, so I can't judge. But I doubt if many look like you."

"We come out in all shapes and sizes."

"Well, there it is," he said. "She was a loathsome woman, but she's dead now."

He paused and drank his wine. I could think of nothing to say, yet I felt that he wanted me to speak.

"She's dead now," he repeated slowly. "And perhaps . . . perhaps it would do no harm."

I sat up in my chair.

"You mean there's still a chance you'll give us permission?" I asked.

"How you do rush your fences!" he exclaimed with a smile. "I mean – to be precise – that my refusal is no longer definite. I would like to hear more about the project."

"You've read my treatment. What more can I tell you – except that the film will be well directed? You may have heard of André Calmann."

"I may have, but the name means nothing to me now. You forget that it's twenty years since I was last in England."

He leaned forward to fill up our glasses. Then he sat back and stared dully at the candles. He seemed no longer interested. He had withdrawn into himself again.

"Can you think of any questions you'd like to ask me?" I suggested hopefully.

With an effort he moved his eyes toward me, away from the candle. "There is just one question," he said. "When you came out here, what were your terms of reference?"

"My terms of reference?"

"Let me put it another way. When I refused to answer their letters and cables it must presumably have occurred to your film friends that I was not, shall we say, wildly enthusiastic for a film about Daphne Moore to be made. Is that correct?"

"Yes," I said, trying to disguise my excitement.

"Did they rely on you to persuade me solely with the aid of your still youthful charm?"

"No," I said, grinning. Here it comes, I thought.

"There were other methods of persuasion?" he suggested with a little chuckle.

"Certainly."

"How much?" he asked suddenly.

He noticed my surprise at the directness of his question and laughed. When he laughed all his face puckered up, and he looked quite young.

"Listen, David, as you can imagine, the whole idea of this film fills me with distaste. But, as you may have heard, this farm is not doing well. I don't want to go into details, and it's not Bill's fault. The fact remains we're losing money, and I'm not a rich man. For Bill's sake – no, that's unfair – for both our sakes I'd be prepared to swallow my pride, to let myself be portrayed on the screen as the lover of that terrible woman if, I repeat if, it were worthwhile. So I come back to my simple question, David. How much?"

"Five hundred pounds."

"Chicken feed. Out of the question. Your friends will have to do better than that."

He paused while Luku removed our plates. Luku and the cook were probably the only houseboys they had. Here, it seemed insufficient. In England, most people would consider it luxury.

"Just supposing I had accepted your overmodest offer," Norman asked, "could you have produced half a thousand like a rabbit from a hat?"

"I could have written you a check on the local bank."

"Tonight?"

"Yes."

"I haven't sat so close to five hundred pounds for a long time. It makes me feel quite dizzy. And I suppose there might be more?"

"There might be," I said.

Now that we had got down to business I realized that I was the last person Stonor should have sent to deal with the man. I lacked not only the ruthlessness and cunning but the inclination to beat him down. I had to remind myself constantly where my loyalty lay.

"Supposing the sum were a thousand – a far rounder, prettier sum," Norman continued. "Then I would be prepared at least to consider giving my consent. Could you write out a check for a thousand? Or would your pen wilt in your nerveless hand?"

"I would have to refer back to London," I said, hating myself for the lie.

"Then refer back. Let the air sing with your reference."

"Supposing I'm empowered to offer you a thousand? When could you give me your decision?"

"Christmas Eve. Bill particularly wants you to dine with us on Christmas Eve. Please do. We'll have great fun, and we can go on to the club afterward."

"I'd love to."

"Speaking of the club reminds me . . . I suppose your film company wouldn't be willing to forward me a small sum of money – say, fifty pounds – in expectation of my consent? Don't I seem to remember from my days in the theater the magic word 'option'?"

"I don't quite see . . ."

"The sad fact is that I have a few debts in the neighborhood," he said, interrupting me gently. "I receive not a penny more from my investments in England until January the first. Fifty pounds would clear my debts, and I would be able to walk into the club on Christmas Eve with my head held as high as my infirmities permit."

"What if you finally decide to refuse consent?"

"I would return the money on January the second."

I thought for a moment. Surely Stonor's company could risk fifty pounds.

"I can lend you the money," I said.

"My dear man! Now?"

"Yes."

I took the checkbook out of my breast pocket.

"Life offers few more beautiful spectacles than a check-book held in generous hands," he murmured, as I wrote out the check. "Generous, though somewhat grubby," he added.

As I handed him the check I saw that the back of my hand was stained with grease that must have come from the car.

"I'm most grateful," he said. "I shall practice head-lifting exercises every morning. Shall we go into the next room for coffee? I have some good Armagnac."

He held the door open for me, and we wandered back into the living room. The pressure lamps seemed almost exhausted. Their light was dim, and their hissing had softened to an almost inaudible whisper. But when Norman rattled their plungers up and down they revived and hissed at each other brightly. Norman lit the spirit flame under the glass beaker and watched the water begin to bubble. Luku had already brought in a Cona and some coffee cups.

"Before we settle down I'd like to wash my hands," I said.

"Literally or euphemistically?"

"Both."

He opened a door at the far end of the room.

"At least old age has not brought me that inconvenience," he said. "You go right to the end of the corridor and it's on the left. Right to the end," he called after me.

As I closed the door behind me I realized that I ought to have taken one of the lamps. The corridor was in complete darkness. For a moment I thought of turning back. Then I decided that my eyes would soon get used to the dark. I moved forward slowly, touching the left wall with my hand. I groped along the corridor for what seemed like ten yards, stroking the wall. Then my hand brushed against the knob of a door. I opened the door cautiously and looked in.

The room was narrow and bare. In the right-hand corner was a mattress strewn with blankets. The only light came from the fire. Kneeling in front of the fire was a little native girl. She was naked, and she was stroking her small breasts, her hands moving in slow upward movements. Her body was beautifully slender. Her skin was smooth, and gleamed in the firelight as if it had been polished. The room was heavy with the warm smell of a young animal.

Though she must have known the door had opened she did not look around. After a moment she said a few words in Swahili. Her voice was soft and inviting. When I made no reply she turned around. In sudden terror she covered her breasts with her hands and leaped up and rushed to the far corner of the room and stood with her back to me, her whole body quivering. I shut the door quickly.

I then remembered that I had a box of matches in my pocket. By the light of a match I saw that I was only halfway down the corridor. There was a candle burning in the lavatory. I took it with me to help me get back to the living room. I decided that in order to save us both embarrassment I would not tell Norman that I had seen the girl. She would tell him after I had gone. Though he might not appreciate my tact, at least he would understand the reason for it. If he wanted to tell me about the girl there was nothing to stop him doing so.

I found Norman pouring out Armagnac into two large *ballons*.

"This would have been the last bottle, but for your kind loan," he said. "I can now go to the Indian grocery in town and look Mr. Sutterjee straight in his odious eye and order another. You've been most kind."

His gratitude made me feel awkward.

"Have you been to India?" I asked.

"Never, but I'd like to. The nearest I got was when I was in the embassy in Baghdad. I wanted to spend my leave on the Northwest Frontier. But I was recalled."

"What made you decide to retire from the Foreign Service?" I asked casually.

He stared down in silence at the liquid he was swirling around in his glass.

"I'd got quite a long way up the tree," he said, after a pause. "I was high enough up to see the topmost branches, and they didn't interest me. I suppose I lacked ambition."

Even before he forced his eyes toward me I knew that he was lying.

"Have you any particular ambition?" he asked me.

"I'd like to make a perfect film without any concession to the box office."

"Tell me more. I love to hear people talking about things they really care about."

He settled himself comfortably in his chair to listen. I could see that he was pleased with himself for having diverted my attention from his own past. And thus it was for the rest of the evening. He was no longer withdrawn. But if the conversation touched him personally he was evasive, and if I tried to corner him he would smile at me blandly and parry my question with a lie. He would lie neatly and politely without making any effort to convince me. "Here comes another lie," his attitude seemed to say. "I'm telling it because I don't want to answer your question." When we talked about books or painting, however, he spoke with eager sincerity, and he was prepared to discuss the problems of existence in general terms so long as no direct reference was made to his own private life.

Gradually, the Armagnac made him less cautious. I felt that part of him now longed to tell me the truth about his past. Though discretion still held him on a leash, he was beginning to strain forward to reach his secret territory. At last he gave me a glimpse of what lay hidden.

He had led the conversation toward the subject of human conduct.

"Do you think there are any fixed rules?" I asked, to give him an opening.

"I'm not certain," he said slowly. "I'm the wrong person to ask about ethics, and there's nothing new about what I believe. I suppose Aristotle may have been the first person to say it. Do you remember what he says about the 'man of great mind'? He won't run risks for small ends. He won't exert himself in small things because he despises them. But he will run a great risk. And at a time of great danger he will be reckless of his life."

He tilted back his head to drink the last drops of Armagnac in his glass.

"I don't think it matters so much what you do in little things," he said. "Minor transgressions, the small faults of vanity or lust, can be forgiven. But when the great moment comes, if ever such an opportunity is granted to you in your life, then you must behave impeccably."

He leaned back in his chair. Suddenly he looked exhausted, and I stood up to leave.

The rain had stopped, but the road was still slippery. As I drove slowly back to the Rest House I reckoned that Stonor should be pleased with me. I had a good chance now of getting Norman's consent to the film, and I was going on safari in three days' time. As for Norman himself, his behavior was outrageous in many ways, yet there was something about him that I liked. My thoughts began to flit as haphazardly as the night birds darting through the beams of the headlights.

Mary Leyton had said that Bill had an instinct about people. And, after all, Bill was obviously fond of Norman. Somewhere beneath the layers of poise and evasion there must be a real person. I had even seen that person for an instant when Norman spoke of what he believed.

I wondered if the "great moment" in his life had occurred during the 1914 war. Then, he could have stayed and should have stayed in the Foreign Service. Instead, he had made every effort to get into the trenches, and I knew that he had indeed been "reckless of his life." Perhaps that was the "great moment" he would never forget.

*

I was glad to see the lights of the Rest House through the trees. I did not then know how much gladder I would be to see those lights three weeks later.

## 10

When we saw the lights of the Rest House, Tim Curry and I had been driving in silence for several hours. During the eighteen days of the safari we had finished every possible morsel of conversation, picking the bones bare as we sat by the campfire or trudged through the sticky red earth of the Ruaha Valley.

Never trust the tough, shy type of man to retain his diffidence on a safari. Over a pink gin at the pub his bashfulness may be endearing. Put a Mannlicher into his hands in the jungle and see what happens. Gone with the first shot is that shy charm. Gone is your gentle companion. And in his place there stands a bluff, domineering stranger glowing with pride, a hearty senior prefect who has just scored a touchdown.

" 'Ware crocs," Tim would bellow as we waded across some murky river. "Keep heading upstream or the current will get you. Lost a boy here only a month ago."

"Wakey, wakey. Rise and shine," he would cry, as he playfully shook my camp bed an hour before dawn. "Upsa-daisy."

But though his heartiness was almost unbearable, his good nature remained constant, unimpaired by the senior prefect. He was kind and even-tempered, and he needed to be, for it soon became evident to both of us that I was the wrong man to take on safari. I resent the need to beware of crocodiles or to sleep with a loaded gun beside my bed. I am not the right man to send out toward dusk in pursuit of a wounded hyena. I do not feel happy crawling across a tree trunk fifty feet above a raging torrent. Most wild animals fill me with terror. I would prefer not to shoot the innocuous ones.

The days passed very slowly. However, I discovered some

excellent locations for a film, and by the time I returned I had made notes for an African story in which Miss Grant and Master Calpe might conceivably display such talents as they possessed.

"Susan will be mad at me for being three days late," Tim said, breaking the silence. "But how was I to know we'd break two sets of springs?"

"How indeed?" I murmured in sympathy. We had had to wait three days beside a malarial swamp while a spare set was procured from the garage in Iringa.

We found Susan Curry drinking port in the bar with Ma Bolting.

"We were organizing a search party for you two," Ma Bolting cried. "When you hadn't turned up on Sunday we thought you'd been trampled to death by elephants. On Monday you'd been savaged by lions. On Tuesday it was hyenas. Wednesday was leopard day. And it wasn't till yesterday we heard you'd bust your springs. I've been simply distracted with anxiety. You'd neither of you settled your bar accounts. What's more, I bet you've had nothing to eat all evening."

"Right in one," Tim said.

"There! What did I tell you, Susan? I suppose you want me to find you a bite?"

Tim glanced quickly at his wife. He was diffident again.

"I've already eaten," Susan said. "But you both look hungry."

"I'll get you food in ten minutes," Ma Bolting announced. "Keep the part where you rescued each other from a rhino till I get back."

She bustled away toward the kitchen. Susan Curry walked over to the door and made certain it was closed. Then she moved to the far corner of the room and beckoned to us mysteriously.

"Quick," she whispered. "Before she comes back there's something I've got to tell you both."

"Fire away," Tim said.

Her eyes were bright with excitement.

"Barry Leyton's found out," she said.

I felt a twinge of fear as if I had been the guilty person.

"Found out what?" Tim asked.

"About Mary and Bill. I'm almost certain of it."

"Almost?"

"Barry came over to our place earlier this evening," she began.

Her voice trembled as she told us about his visit. She was obviously enjoying her moment of importance. We were told what dress she was wearing; we were given an account of her thoughts when she saw a car – a station wagon of sorts, it was – approaching her house at sundown; we learned of her fear that Barry would ask for whisky when there was none in the house; we heard it all – beginning and middle and end.

The facts were simple. Barry Leyton had driven over to see Tim. He had been disappointed to learn that Tim was still away on safari, but he had come into the living room for a drink with Susan. He had seemed distracted, and his manner had been abrupt, almost rude. Over his second drink he had begun to talk about Norman Hartleigh.

"I've detested that sort all my life," Barry said. "If I were the District Officer I'd run him out of the country."

"I'm sorry for young Bill," Susan said, watching her guest carefully.

"I'm not sorry for him," Barry said. "He's old enough to know the difference between right and wrong. If he goes about with a man like that he deserves everything that's coming to him. And it may be quite a lot."

Barry finished his drink and stood up.

"All the same you're right in a way," he said. "Hartleigh's the guiltier of the two. He's got some horrible influence over the young man. I wouldn't put it past him to use that influence to get even with a person he disliked. That may be the answer to it all."

Barry then said good-bye quickly and left.

"His eyes were odd and staring," Susan said in conclusion. "I'm almost certain he'd found out."

I looked at Tim. He was still thinking about her story.

"How could he have found out?" I asked. "Who could have told him?"

"One of the boys," Susan answered. "They get to know everything in time."

"Would a boy dare tell him such a thing?"

"It might be the other way around," Tim said slowly. "The boy might not dare to refuse to tell him – if Barry questioned him hard enough. I've heard that Barry can get quite tough."

"Why do you think he drove across to see you?"

"That's just what I've been wondering, and I still can't find the answer."

"I hope young Bill doesn't turn up at the club tomorrow night," Susan said. "The Christmas Eve dance is our big event of the year, and we don't want any trouble."

"They both came last year," Tim muttered.

"I'm dining with them tomorrow night," I said, "and so far as I know they'll both be coming again this year."

"You must stop them. We don't want any trouble," Susan repeated primly.

Suddenly her smugness irritated me.

"How can I possibly stop them?" I asked. "Why should I stop them if they want to enjoy themselves? I suggest that one of you try to prevent Barry Leyton coming since you're so certain he's going to cause trouble."

"But he's the innocent party."

"That remains to be proved."

"Look, David, I'll make a bargain with you," Tim said, intervening quietly. "If you warn young Bill to be careful, I'll do my best to see that Barry doesn't make a row."

"Agreed," I said as Ma Bolting came back into the bar.

And thus it was left.

As soon as I arrived at Imunda the following evening I saw that both Norman and Bill were determined to visit the club that night. Norman was wearing an old dinner jacket which the passing years had tinged with green. Beneath the single-breasted jacket I could see a faded waistcoat of watered silk with pearl buttons. The corners of a white silk handkerchief protruded from his breast pocket. He had obviously done his best to make himself spruce for the occasion. Now and then he would glance toward Bill with a smile of pride.

Bill had the overclean, oversmart appearance of a juvenile lead in a film. His pale hair was carefully slicked back, and all his clothes from his gleaming patent leather shoes to his neat black bow tie looked as if they had been bought the previous day. His movements were less spontaneous than usual, as if they were constrained by the importance of his new clothes; but his eyes were shining with excitement. Even the room looked festive. The rafters dripped with paper garlands and bells and lanterns.

"You must pinch my arm for luck," Bill said as he refilled my glass with sherry. "This dinner jacket's brand-new. Norman cabled to Nairobi for the material three weeks ago. The Indian tailor in Iringa only got it finished yesterday."

Bill pulled down the double-breasted jacket and turned around so that I could admire the cut.

"Do you think it's all right?" he asked anxiously. "It's the first I've ever had, and it cost a small fortune, I can tell you."

"I think it's perfect," I said truthfully. "It must have cost all of fifty pounds."

"Not quite," Bill said, laughing.

Norman met my accusing stare without a trace of shame. "Let's go in to dinner," he said. "We don't want to spoil the goose."

★

The dining-room table glittered with tinsel decorations and mounds of red firecrackers. I now understood why I had been invited: I was the excuse for a party. Alone together they would have been embarrassed by the bright display. It is sad enough to feel lonely by yourself; it is worse to feel lonely with a friend. I determined to play my part in their plan. I drank several glasses of South African wine and tried to remember some amusing stories. But I need not have bothered to make an effort; they only needed the presence of a guest to make the evening seem extraordinary. They were both charged with happiness, and their high spirits were infectious. Bill talked excitedly about the farm, and Norman astonished and delighted me with stories of his early days in the Foreign Office. They both shared particular turns of phrase and catchwords as people do who have lived a long time together. It was amusing to hear Bill use long words and Norman break into slang. I was sorry when the meal was over and we wandered back to the living room. I was beginning to dread the dance.

Norman poured us out some Armagnac and disappeared down the corridor. I wondered whether he would stop for a moment to say good night to the native girl. I was alone with Bill, and I remembered my promise to Tim. I was about to speak when Bill gave me my cue.

"I'm just longing for tonight," he said. "Last time I only had a lounge suit. And that isn't really the same thing, is it?"

"Listen, Bill," I said gently. "This is none of my business, but if Mary and Barry Leyton are at the club do please be careful."

I was dismayed to see the anxious look come back into his eyes.

"Why do you say that?" he asked.

"Because I've got a hunch that Barry has begun to suspect."

"So long as he's got no proof – what if he does?"

"He might make a scene."

Bill looked down at his large red hands.

"He'd never dare," he said.

"Bill, don't be a fool. Barry's no coward and he could be tougher than you. Besides, he's got a nasty temper. He might take it out on Mary."

"I promise you that Mary's safe. I swear it," Bill cried vehemently. "I'd never have started if I hadn't been certain of that. I can't explain all of it, but I can tell you this. He's been jealous before I came along, and he's never dared lay a finger against her. He knows if he did she'd leave him."

"What about Norman?"

"I don't get you."

"He might pick a quarrel with Norman."

Suddenly the large hands were clenched so that the knuckles showed white.

"If he attacked Norman in any way," Bill said slowly, "he'd have me to fight, and he knows it."

"Why does he know it?"

"Because one day at the club I heard him make a dirty crack against Norman when he thought I wasn't there, and I told him in those very words."

"I still ask you to be careful."

Bill walked over to me and put his hands on my shoulders.

"I'm an ungrateful bastard," he said. "Thanks for the tip. You were dead right to warn me. I promise I'll be careful. Now, what about some brandy?"

When Norman returned to the room he asked if he could drive to the club in my car.

"Your car is far more comfortable than the truck," he said, "and Bill drives so fast he makes me nervous."

"Not nearly as nervous as your driving makes me," Bill said, grinning at him affectionately. "And if you're not careful I won't drive you home. Come on. Let's finish our drinks. It's time to go. I'll lead the way in the truck."

Though it had not rained all day the road was still muddy.

"Drive cautiously and Bill will slow down to wait for us," Norman said. "I'm terrified of the roads in this country. One slip and you can crash into a ravine. Each time I have to drive alone I pour with sweat. I don't know what I'd do without Bill. I'm so glad you admired his dinner jacket."

"I'm glad you paid off all your debts," I said acidly.

Norman chuckled.

"I did pay a few debts," he said. "But then I remembered how much Bill wanted a dinner jacket. You see, to him it's more than a mere jacket, it's a symbol of something he's longed for."

"Life can offer few greater pleasures than to be generous with another person's money," I said.

"You must never make a remark like that," Norman protested. "It's out of character. You're not a cynic, you're a wild romantic, and you must know it perfectly well. After all, it's what gains you your bread and butter."

"I like to believe I'm a mixture of the two."

"Tell me the story of your last film and I'll decide."

"If you'll remember, you promised to give me your decision tonight about our new film."

"So I did, and so I will before we part."

I imagined that he was waiting for a favorable opportunity to ask for more money.

"There's plenty of time yet," he continued. "Now tell me the story of your last film. How did it start?"

His technique for changing the conversation was blatantly obvious, but he had given me an excellent dinner, and, after all, it was Christmas Eve, so I obediently began to tell the story of "The Second Daughter" while he heckled me cheerfully and the car slid through the darkness.

I finished the story as we turned off into the side road that led to the club.

"It's really quite good," he said in a surprised voice. "I thought they only made films like . . . I mean, films that played down to the lowest in the audience."

He had been about to say "like your story about Daphne Moore." I looked at him. He was peering ahead and his hands were moving restively.

"Are you sure those are the lights of the truck ahead of us?" he asked. He had suddenly become nervous.

"Are you sure that's Bill ahead?" he repeated.

"Certain."

"I wish he'd wait for us."

"He's slowing down now."

"That's all right then. We can all three arrive together."

## 12

The club was an assembly of refurbished Nissen huts with two tennis courts and a garage. When I parked my car beside Bill's truck it was eleven-thirty, and the dance had started two hours earlier. We walked up the drive toward the main block. Luckily it was not yet raining. I noticed that Bill was fingering the ends of his bow tie. He, too, had now become nervous.

"They haven't half put on a good show," he muttered as we turned the corner.

Rows of little Japanese lanterns flickered along the concrete terrace. Even an attempt at floodlighting had been made with disused headlights. And into the African night, a phonograph blared music that had sprung from the African continent and was now being wafted back again via Paris, Harlem, and Hollywood. Through the open windows of the reading room, which had been cleared and festooned with paper streamers for the occasion, we could see about thirty couples gliding around on the polished floor. From Iringa to the north and Dodoma way they had come, from Mufindi to the south and beyond Mbeya, prepared to drive several hundreds of miles over wretched roads for the sake of one bright crowded evening. In little huts by the light of kerosene lamps, in farmhouses and in the large brick bungalows of retired officials, while the auxiliary lighting plants chuffed and wheezed, they had put on their best clothes and sallied forth into the darkness along greasy sodden roads, prepared to spend more money than they could afford for the sake of this one evening which they would discuss for months afterward, rehearsing each event, describing yet again the dress and mannerisms of

one and the gaiety or drunkenness of another. The Christmas dance would be remembered as a comet streaking across
the monotony of their lives.

We pushed our way into the crowded hall. All the women
were in long dresses of a kind, I noticed. Most of the men
wore dinner jackets, the rest blue suits.

"Let's head for the bar," Norman said.

The barroom was even more crowded than the hall. We
moved toward the far corner where two large red-faced men
with white mustaches were leaning against the counter,
ordering drinks for the two women who stood behind them.

"Evening, Hartleigh," the taller of the two men said curtly.

Norman took my arm.

"I want to introduce David Brent, who's visiting the
Southern Highlands," he said. "This is Brigadier Cobb, our
secretary."

After that it was inevitable that I should be introduced to
the Brigadier's wife and to her companion, who was married
to Colonel Anstey, the other tall man. Fortunately, they were
all determined to be affable. I saw the two women look for an
instant at Norman's waistcoat and then fix their stares on Bill.

"You'll find sufficient officers of field rank up here to staff
an army corps," Norman murmured to me as I ordered three
brandies.

The Brigadier's wife was now whispering something to
her friend. Mrs. Anstey giggled and looked at Bill with greater
interest. Bill blushed and moved uneasily toward me.

"Do you mind if I don't wait for my drink?" he blurted out
suddenly. "I want to see the dancing."

"I'll come with you," Norman said quickly. "We can leave
our drinks till we get back."

Norman smiled at me apologetically and followed Bill out
of the room. Seeing that I was now alone, the Colonel, who
looked stouter and more prosperous than the Brigadier, drew
me into his group and introduced me to a politician called
Hooker.

"He's one of these M.P.s from England out to visit the

country," the Colonel explained in a loud whisper. "His plane's broken down on an airfield a hundred miles away, so I've taken him off to my place to show him around a bit. After all, I couldn't leave the chap stranded over Christmas in a tin shed without even a decent latrine. And he looks as if he could do with a bit of feeding up."

Hooker was a thin, pallid man with refined features. He was wearing a crumpled gabardine suit and an Old School tie. His physique had evidently been unable to cope with the Colonel's generosity. He was now consuming a glass of club champagne with mild distaste. I wondered why he had given up all pretense of enjoying the evening. I soon found out.

"What has your government done for the sisal growers?" the Brigadier was asking him rhetorically. "Nothing, if you'll permit me to say so."

"Your entire approach to the groundnut scheme was wrong from the outset," his host added. "If you wanted groundnuts, you should have subsidized private farmers like us who've been out here twenty years. Instead, you've made a damn-fool mess of it."

Unsuitable background music to their conversation was now being provided by the phonograph on the dance floor. The full richness of the "Blue Danube" waltz swayed behind their clipped words.

"You just don't understand the natives," the Brigadier said. "Now, brother black is a fine chap when you get to know him, but he's got to be kept in his place. Let brother black think he's our equal and you'll have every white woman raped from Kilimanjaro to Victoria Falls."

"Extremely interesting," Hooker murmured in a flat, delicate voice. He was evidently growing tired of the principle of collective responsibility.

"Worse than that," the Colonel added. "You'll have the blacks thinking they own the place."

"Tell me, Hooker, if you get into power next time – and it's a pretty big 'if' – precisely what will your government do to prevent colored infiltration into the Southern Highlands?"

Hooker gazed at his hospitable tormentors seemingly without interest. Then he cleared his throat.

"I expect," he replied in clear, scholastic tones, "sweet Fanny Adams."

I was watching the faces of the two wives, who were uncertain whether they should join the throaty laughter of their husbands, when I heard my name called and turned around. It was Mary Leyton. She was wearing a black strapless dress, so plain and well cut that it made the other women look garish and shoddy. As if to atone for being more expensively dressed than her neighbors, or perhaps to accentuate the effect, she wore no jewelry. Her chestnut-brown hair fell waving to her shoulders. Her eyes seemed alive with an intense and secret happiness.

"Dr. Livingstone, I presume," she said. "I'm tired of dancing. Let's take our drinks outside."

We walked to the end of the garden and stood together in the moonlight watching the mist rising from the plain, while ripples of dance music lapped against our ears.

"I'm sinking," Mary said in mock remorse. "You must forgive me."

"For what?"

"That Dr. Livingstone joke. I can still feel the prickles. But out here we all get like that in time. And who cares? The point of life isn't to be bright. The point is to be happy when you can."

She gazed up at the sky and laughed.

"Why do I find it so easy to talk to you?" she asked.

"Because I'm an outsider up here. I don't matter, so you feel safe with me."

"I'm not sure about that."

"The passing stranger gets told things the next-door neighbor never hears."

"You're no longer a stranger."

Faintly we could hear the lilt of "Buttons and Bows."

"'Don't bury me in the far prairie where the cactus tickles my toes,'" she quoted dreamily. Then she turned to me defiantly and said: "I wouldn't mind where I was buried so long as I'd lived with Bill for twenty years."

She looked up at me like a guilty schoolchild, her eyes begging me not to scold her, not to laugh or be unsympathetic.

"Twenty years is a long time," I said tritely.

"But, you see, I really know him, and I love all of him. I know every corner of his mind. I know his obstinacy. I know his loyalty and tenderness. I know how easily his little vanity can be hurt. I know his fears and ambitions. And every day I love him more. And he's got a wonderfully soft mouth," she added, as if that settled the matter.

"Weren't you once in love with Barry?"

She stared down into the valley in silence.

"Weren't you?" I repeated softly.

"As a man, yes. Never as a person. You see . . . No, I can't explain. Just take it that I only found out too late."

"You found out that he was a sadist."

She was silent, but I knew from her face that I was right.

"Does the kind of scene we had that night after dinner occur often?"

"No, thank God."

I handed her a cigarette. I could think of nothing to say. Suddenly Mary shivered.

"Let's go in," she said. "It's cold."

As we walked back we saw Barry Leyton striding up and down the terrace. His scowl disappeared when he saw that I was Mary's partner.

"It's past midnight," he said. "Happy Christmas to you both."

Though his face was flushed with drink, his movements were light and neat as he moved quickly toward Mary and took her arm.

"I've been waiting to have a dance with my wife," he said.

I followed them into the main room. The floor was still crowded. Bill was dancing with Susan Curry, who was wearing a beige dress with lace frills. They noticed me standing by the door and came up to me. I asked Susan to dance, and

Bill relinquished her gratefully to my care; he had seen Mary come in with Barry.

"Is all well?" Susan whispered in my ear as we shuffled around the room. She smelled of lavender and moth balls.

"I warned Bill," I said. "Did Tim talk to Barry?"

"That's just it. I don't think he's had a chance yet."

"Then he'd better move quickly because Barry's had a lot to drink."

"I'll tell him after this dance."

Susan danced well but conservatively so that, bad dancer though I am, I was soon able to concentrate on what was going on around us. Bill had now joined the small group by the phonograph. Now and then he would look at Mary gliding smoothly in the arms of her husband. Norman was at the far end of the room talking to Ma Bolting, who was sitting disapprovingly erect and massive in a dress of plum-colored velvet. Mary called out to him gaily as she passed and Norman waved to her happily. But Barry made no sign of recognition. Tim was dancing nervously with Mrs. Anstey, who had shut her eyes in blissful abandon.

"Silly old cow," Susan said. "As if Tim would even look at another woman."

I was glad when the record was finished because I had begun to feel thirsty, and the atmosphere of the room with its undercurrents of emotion was beginning to make me feel claustrophobic. Susan said she would join me in the bar after she had rescued Tim. I stood for a while on the terrace inhaling gulps of fresh air. Then I strolled away to get a drink.

13

The only person I knew in the bar was Jack Prescott, the District Officer. I had met him with Tim on my unfortunate safari. He was a good-natured man who was neither as conceited nor as stupid as he looked. I was delighted to see him, for at least he was a link with the outside world. The problems of the Aruna end of the Southern Highlands were beginning to oppress me.

"Merry Christmas, I don't think," Prescott said as I came up to him. "At least not for yours truly. I'll give you six bottles of genuine whisky if you take that Swede off my hands."

"What Swede?"

"*The* Swede, *the* Swede. Thank God, there's only one of him. He's a professor of photography, whatever that may mean. For heaven knows what reason, he's a V.I.P., and I've been landed with him. Six whole bottles," the District Officer said, glaring furiously at a stout white-faced man who was sidling toward us.

The man had an innocent, unlined face and pale watery blue eyes, and he was dressed in a very dirty blue tweed suit. He was obviously the professor.

"Six whole bottles," he said in a quiet sad voice. "Is this not the name of an English ditty tune? Six whole bottles standing on a wall. You sing this at Christmas, perhaps?"

"Yes," Prescott said, "we do."

"I do not leave you just now because I am annoyed," he continued, "but my stomach is not good today. Not at all good," he said, turning to me kindly in explanation. "The doctor thinks I eat something to poison me. But surely," he asked, swinging around to his host, "surely your food is wholesome?"

"I hope so," Prescott said grimly.

"I could have slept this afternoon. But I wait to take a photograph of the native girls you promised me. And then they do not come."

"Six whole bottles," Prescott said.

"Standing on a wall," the professor chimed in. "For two months on the coast I have natives but no sun. Now I have little sun and no natives."

"Brent here works in films, and he's living in a Rest House on one of the most photogenic properties in the area," Prescott said hopefully.

"But without natives it will look very dull."

"There are dozens of natives where Brent is."

"But why do they wear these European trousers? I can see I must buy scarves in the market to drape around them. I think I should now leave you again."

"You see what I mean," Prescott said as his guest ambled away.

The bar had run out of whisky so we ordered brandies and began to discuss the problems of nationalism and color in East Africa. Our wisdom seemed to grow more profound with each round of drinks. Presently, I noticed that Prescott was leading the conversation toward more local affairs. I had the impression that he wanted to ask me something but hesitated to do so. Yet when the question came I was startled. His face suddenly changed. He was no longer an amiable drinking companion; he was an alert official.

"You've seen quite a bit of Hartleigh and Bill Wayne, haven't you?" he asked.

"I've met them two or three times," I replied cautiously. He glanced down at his glass.

"I'm not much concerned with what goes on in that house of theirs," he said in a voice cold with distaste, "but I don't want trouble in my district."

"Why should there be trouble?"

"You know why. The Currys have told you."

"Do you listen to every rumor?"

"Yes, I do. And then I check up for myself. Young Wayne will get it in the neck if he's not careful, and I may not be able to stop it. This is a rough country."

"That's the second time I've been told that. But it's not true. The conditions are rough – not the people."

"You're wrong in one respect. I've been out here for twenty years, and I can tell you this. If a husband finds out that another man has been playing around with his wife he doesn't search for the nearest solicitor and he doesn't rush to the divorce courts."

"What does he do?"

"You write films. You can guess. And remember – I may not arrive in time to stop it."

Prescott slid off the bar stool.

"I must go and dance," he said.

"Just one moment," I said. "Precisely why have you told me this?"

"Because you can help by passing it on. You like at least two of the people concerned."

"What makes you think so?"

"Your defensive attitude when I asked you the question. So long, Brent."

I stayed in the bar, hoping that Norman would appear so that I could find out his decision about the film and go home to bed. I was now almost certain that he would accept our offer of a thousand pounds. As I was finishing my drink Barry Leyton came into the bar with Mrs. Anstey and Brigadier Cobb. Barry strode toward me. At first I only noticed that he was drunk. His bloodshot eyes peered at me from out of a mottled face. Then I saw that his fingers were quivering in the effort to control the passionate rage that was rising in him.

"Have you seen Mary?" he asked thickly.

"No, I'm afraid not."

"I can't think where she's got to," he muttered, scowling at me in suspicion. "I've been looking for her everywhere."

He turned away from me abruptly and joined a group of his friends who had gathered at the other end of the bar, near the door. He picked up a double brandy and drained it in a gulp.

"More all around," he ordered.

At that particular moment Norman walked into the bar. His hair was a little disheveled, and his dinner jacket now hung open showing his old-fashioned waistcoat. I waved to him, but he did not see me. We were separated by the length of the crowded room. He stood perfectly still, looking around at the faces nearest him. I was sure that he was trying to find Bill. I began to move toward him. Perhaps because of his unusual appearance, perhaps because of some herd instinct of hostility, the room became suddenly quiet. I was about to call out to him when Barry swung around on his bar stool and saw Norman staring vaguely toward him.

"Get out," Barry said. "We don't like your sort in here."

There was complete silence. Every head was turned toward Norman.

Norman did not move. It was as if the shock had paralyzed him. Then he clenched his fists and slowly raised his arms in a trembling gesture. For one ghastly moment I thought he was going to attack Barry, who was looking at him with a smile of contempt. Then, with a shudder, Norman's hands fell to his sides, and he turned away with the jerky movements of a clockwork doll and shuffled out of the bar.

Barry's laugh jarred the silence like a gunshot. A few titters arose from the quiet room. I paid quickly for my drinks and hurried out after Norman. I could still hear Barry's drunken laughter as I pushed my way down the corridor into the hall. I looked into the dance room, hoping to find Bill, but he was not there. I walked to the end of the terrace. I could see the garden clearly in the bright moonlight. Neither Norman nor Bill was there. I turned back in the direction of the car park. As I walked down the concrete path that led to the drive I saw what looked like a small earring lying on the shining surface. I stooped down to pick it up. It was a pearl button.

14

I found Norman sitting in the front of his truck. An opened bottle of brandy was held between his knees. When he saw me he made a desperate effort to smile.

"The club brandy tastes of tin," he said, "so I thought I'd sneak out to my Remy Martin. Can I offer you a drink?"

"No thanks."

"Are you on your way home?"

His voice was as unsteady as his hands.

"Shortly," I said.

He leaned forward and looked carefully into my face. "So you've heard," he said.

"I was there."

His face sagged. He looked old and broken, but he still made an effort to speak lightly as if nothing had happened.

"Could you be very kind and find Bill?" he said. "Don't tell him about that nasty little incident. Just tell him that I feel tired and wish to go home."

"Have you any idea where Bill is?"

"Dancing, I expect."

"Apart from the bar, there's no corner of the club where he might have gone for a quiet drink?"

"None that I know of."

I walked back to the club buildings and looked through the open windows of the long room where they were now dancing the Lambeth Walk. Bill was not there. I searched for him throughout the club – even in the lavatories. As I came into the hall for a last look I met Ma Bolting and Tim Curry. Neither of them had seen Bill during the last hour, but both of them had already heard a distorted version of the scene in the bar.

"Where's Hartleigh?" Tim asked after Ma Bolting had left us to dance with Brigadier Cobb.

"Waiting in his truck. There's nothing for it. I shall have to drive him home."

"God, I'd like to wring that young man's neck."

"So would I just at this moment. But if you see him, tell him that I've driven Norman home and tell him to steer clear of Barry Leyton. You can add that I've got a special message for him from the District Officer. That should damp his ardor."

"I'll lay it on thick," Tim said.

I said good night and returned to the car park.

Norman had not moved since I left him. He did not even turn his head as I came up to the truck window.

"You haven't found him," he said.

"No. But it can't be helped. I can easily drive you home."

"It's miles out of your way."

"It's a fine night, and I don't feel tired."

I opened the door of the truck and he got out stiffly, clutching the bottle of brandy in his left hand. I was glad that I had parked my car beside the truck. I helped him into the car and started the engine.

"Can't we wait a little longer for Bill?" he asked. "He'll be worried when he finds I've gone."

"Let him be worried for a change," I said grimly.

"He may search for me all night."

"He won't. I've left a message for him."

"Thank you. That's all I was fussing about."

Norman was silent until we reached the end of the club drive and turned onto the road. I had noticed that the bottle of brandy was half empty, yet when he began to talk his voice showed no trace of drink. He spoke quietly and clearly, without any hesitation, in a flat, expressionless tone. Only the rhythm of his sentences showed that his mind had changed as the inhibitions were lifted. He was sitting motionless, his eyes fixed on the road ahead, musing, as if he were alone.

"Cruel, not to be able to learn from experience," the dead voice said. "Cruel, the moment you realize you've wasted half your life and it's all your fault. Again and again you've flung the chips of time carelessly onto the green baize cloth. And now, there you sit, fingering the few plaques left, while the wheel spins and spins without purpose. You can't leave the table, you can't stop playing, you can't even stop hoping that for once your number will be lucky. So there you sit watching, while the ball rolls around the dark well."

For a while he was silent, and I thought he had gone to sleep. But when I turned my head I saw that his eyes were open, and presently he tilted the bottle to his lips. A thin rain had begun to fall. The road was dangerous, and I was tired, and I can remember nothing more of the journey until we reached the turning to Imunda. The jagged signboard somehow prompts my memory so that I can hear his voice and the creak of the windshield wiper.

"So you must find an escape," he was saying. "And, for most, drink is easier to get than dope. And soon euphoria descends like a blessing. The lost chips no longer matter. You can make more if you choose or you can leave the table if you wish. Memories of degradation and foolishness, of opportunities missed and friends betrayed, are softened. Nothing is of importance now except your mind which, released from grossness and guilt, soars happily about the present, patrolling the area for future operations. You know all things and you understand all things. You are all-seeing and all-wise. You are made in God's image. In the morning despair will wake you. But now a fragment of divinity is glowing in your mind, so that you can perceive the harmony of creation and the insignificance of its individual notes."

Suddenly he laughed.

"Jehovah minor, you sit sozzling in a shabby dinner jacket," he said as we stopped in front of his house.

I took my flashlight out of the glove compartment and helped him across the muddy courtyard to the front door.

"Please come in for a drink," he pleaded. "I've still got to give you my decision. Please come in."

The two pressure lamps in the living room had hissed themselves to extinction. I lit a kerosene lamp while Norman threw some logs on the glowing ashes.

"Whisky's on the sideboard," he said, sitting down in the big armchair by the chimney piece. "Help yourself. None for me. I'll stick to brandy. Never mix grape and grain."

I poured myself a drink and sat down in the armchair opposite him. Faintly in the distance I could hear the drums beating in the native village near the turning to Imunda.

"There's an 'ngoma," Norman said. "They're dancing as well tonight."

For a while he watched me carefully as if he were trying to read my thoughts.

"When I delayed my decision you thought I was going to ask for more money, didn't you?" he asked quietly.

"Yes."

"I hoped that was what you'd think. I didn't want to spoil your evening with the one word 'No.'"

I stared at him.

"You mean you'll turn down a thousand pounds?"

"I'd turn down two thousand."

"Was that your decision before . . ."

"It was my decision before you came here to dine."

I searched his face to discover if he was playing some trick to be offered more money. But there was no flicker of guile in his steady gaze. For once he was being frank. He meant what he said.

"I think you're mad," I broke out.

"And ungrateful too. Go on. Say it."

"Gratitude has nothing to do with it."

"It has in a way. You've been very kind to me, and I would have liked to help you. But I can't let you make that film."

Suddenly I remembered all the miles I had traveled and all the efforts I had made to persuade him. I forgot that he had been humiliated in the club. I forgot that he was trying to drink himself into oblivion. I was only bitterly conscious that I had failed in my mission.

"I can't," he repeated. "And that's an end to it."

Then I lost my temper.

"Why not, for heaven's sake?" I asked. "We can change your precious name in the film. We can call you plain Smith if you like. It's not your name we want, it's the character. It's a young, charming diplomat we want, with a career ahead of him. And just tell me who in the whole world cares two hoots that it was really Norman Hartleigh who slept with Daphne Moore? Who cares?"

For the first time since the afternoon I had called on him I saw a glint of anger in his eyes.

"I care," he said. "And I'll tell you why."

## 15

Norman's story began at the period when he first met Daphne Moore. At least the framework of my treatment had been correct. Norman Hartleigh had indeed obtained leave of absence from the Foreign Office to fight in Flanders. During the first eight years after the war he had indeed risen surprisingly high for his age in the Service; he was head of the Western department. To amuse himself in his spare time he had certainly written a comedy called "Wine for Caroline," and a mutual friend had given it to Cole Edwards, the manager, who had taken it to Daphne Moore.

So far my film story had been accurate, but my estimate of Daphne Moore's importance in London in 1927 had, it seemed, been mistaken. After three plays she had starred in had flopped in quick succession, Daphne Moore had announced her retirement from the stage in 1925. Her agent had provided her with an excuse that was certain to appeal to her public: now that her husband was dead she must devote her time to looking after her son, Peter, who was then eleven years old.

This excuse did not impress Cole Edwards. He knew that she had never taken much interest in her son – except for reasons of publicity; he also had good reason to know about her failures, for he had been financially involved in them. He therefore hesitated a long time before taking Norman's play to her. But the title role called for precisely the qualities that Daphne Moore possessed. It was a "stagey" part requiring flamboyance and, above all, poise and perfect timing. Moreover, there was no doubt that Daphne Moore had once had a great following. Cole Edwards went down to her Jacobean house in Kent. Her enthusiasm lent him confidence; but he was still uncertain as he sat with Norman at his usual corner table in the Ritz, waiting for Daphne to join them.

Daphne's maid had telephoned to say that Miss Moore would be half an hour late. Norman sipped his sherry and watched Cole Edwards' stubby white fingers kneading his bread into little white pills. Cole was a squat, plump little man of sixty with a passion for young chorus girls. His eyes were now darting nervously around the room.

"There she is," Cole said.

Norman looked around. For a moment Daphne Moore stood poised in the entrance while the head waiter glided swiftly toward her. Then she gave him a brilliant smile of gratitude, as if he had released her from perpetual immobility, moved her arm to acknowledge the greetings of some friends at a nearby table, and turned away toward the corner table.

As he saw her moving toward them across the room Norman was certain that Cole's doubts had been unjustified, and his heart lifted. At the age of fourteen he had been taken by his parents to see her in a matinee. This was the same face that he remembered, the same vitality, the same magic. This was the woman for his play. He was in such a daze of excitement that he was hardly aware of Cole's introduction. It was not until they sat down that he dared to look at her again. Then he had to force his lips into a smile as he answered the polite question she had asked him. He hoped that his eyes had not shown his dismay when he first saw her face a yard away, for the features that combined to form an appearance of radiant charm at a distance – the uptilted nose, the heavily fringed blue eyes, the generous mouth – seen at close range were gross and disjointed. The nose was fleshy, the eyes faded, the mouth flabby. He was gazing into the face of a coarse woman past middle age.

He was glad when she turned to Cole Edwards. He listened while they talked. She had a contralto voice, full and rich enough for Racine; but she talked in quick jerky sentences. You expected a sonorous period; you got plain jargon. The contrast was diverting. And soon Norman found he was joining in their laughter as she chaffed Cole Edwards about his love affairs. Age had not diminished her vitality, and there was still magic in her voice. Gradually, Norman's attitude changed again. After all, she had looked entrancing from across the room; why not from across the footlights?

When she began to discuss the play he realized that she was shrewd and intelligent. Firmly she pointed out the main weakness of the plot in the second half of the last act and put forward her own suggestions. When he defended his version she sailed into the attack.

"You may be England's bright hope as a diplomat," she said, "but you're still a rotten dramatist."

Cole Edwards left them arguing happily. He was now convinced that his choice had been right. Still arguing, Norman and Daphne wandered together across St. James's Park in the bright spring sunshine. (At least my treatment had been right on this point.) The following weekend Norman was asked down to Mullings, the country house in Kent that Daphne's husband had bought five years before he died. And thus their friendship began.

In his ignorance, Norman had supposed that once the final version of the play was written there would be little delay before production. But rehearsals did not start until September. By that time Daphne and Norman enjoyed the easy relationship of old friends. Norman had rewritten the last act, though he had not accepted in full the change that Daphne wanted because he felt it was so drastic that it unbalanced the whole play. But Norman was grateful for her enthusiasm and advice, and he was a little flattered by her affection.

As soon as he had begun to mix with her friends in London he had learned that for several years she had been passionately in love with a young Shakespearean actor who lived in a mews flat she owned in Chelsea and was still her one and only love. Her affection for Norman was obviously on a different plane. This pleased Norman because he was only attracted by women younger than himself. Though he had never been in love, Norman had had several discreet affairs at home and abroad when the opportunity so offered. But he had no intention of becoming entangled with a woman fourteen years older than himself. (In my treatment I had, of course, reduced her age by a few years.) He enjoyed her company, but he pitied the Shakespearean actor.

"Wine for Caroline" opened in the West End in November. Daphne gave a wonderful performance (I knew – I had read the notices), and the play was an immediate success.

Up to the moment of the first night, Norman had told me his story in outline. He now began to describe each scene in detail so that I felt I could almost see the garish drawing room in which Cole Edwards gave his party after the first night.

Daphne and Norman arrived together. They were immediately surrounded by their friends, and superlatives floated around their heads.

"Where's my darling Peter?" Daphne asked suddenly.

Her son Peter was collected from the far end of the room where he was drinking cider with the assistant stage manager, and she embraced him fondly. Peter, who was now fifteen, had been allowed leave from Eton for the night. He was a quiet, well-mannered boy with blond hair and blue eyes that always looked serious. At first he had been shy with Norman, almost hostile, but during the summer holidays he had been less diffident. He was Daphne's only child. During the holidays he spent most of the time alone. There were several children of his own age in the neighborhood, and Daphne frequently urged him to join them, for his quiet presence seemed to irritate her. But he still preferred to wander about the house or to go riding alone on the chestnut pony he adored.

"Many congratulations, sir," he said to Norman.

"Thanks," Norman replied. "But I thought we agreed last holidays you wouldn't call me 'sir.' I'm not an ambassador yet, you know."

"In a few years' time, from what I hear, you will be," Daphne said.

"Nonsense," Norman laughed. "Now you've made the play a success they won't take me seriously. They'll think I'm too flippant."

Daphne took his arm.

"Let's escape into the next room for a moment," she said. "There's something I want to tell you."

Wondering why she had become serious, Norman followed her into Cole's study. She closed the door and turned to face him.

"We've got to be careful," she said.

He looked at her in bewilderment. She was wearing her famous black pearls with a white evening dress that glittered in the light of the desk lamp. She was smiling at him tenderly. But there was more than tenderness in her voice when she spoke. To his amazement Norman detected the soft understanding note of some mutual conspiracy.

"You must have heard the rumors," she said.

"Rumors?"

"My dear, surely you know what our friends are saying all around London?"

"No."

"They're saying that we're lovers."

Only the solemn tone of her voice stopped him from laughing. A friend of his in the Office had indeed warned him that there might be some gossip if he were seen too often in her company. He had listened to the warning with amusement. A girl friend had even suggested to him that Daphne Moore was spreading the rumor deliberately in order to counteract the impression that her charms had faded. This imputation he had ascribed to malice. He could not believe that anyone in their senses would suppose he was her lover because the idea of it seemed so fantastic. He was beginning to realize that he might have been wrong. As he stared at her, he saw Daphne force her lips into a smile.

"Your consternation is hardly flattering, my dear," she said.

Norman made an effort to change his expression.

"I'm proud they should think it," he said, "but I admit I'm

surprised. I thought people knew there was only one love in your life."

She gazed at him reflectively. Her mouth was still framed in a smile, but her eyes were hard.

"Perhaps you underrate your charm compared with Vivian's," she said.

Norman knew that Vivian was the young Shakespearean actor.

"The fact remains – people think we're lovers. Even Vivian's heard it. Of course he was furious, poor sweet. But it's all around London. One more scandal isn't going to damage my career, but it might hurt yours, so I think we'd better be careful. Don't you agree?"

"Perhaps, for a while. But I shall miss so much . . ."

"Don't worry. If we go easy for a month or two the gossip will soon die down and we can be friends again. You see, my dear, Peter and I don't want to lose you. We want you to remain our friend."

"What's Peter got to do with it?"

"He likes you, Norman."

"That's the first time I knew it."

Daphne walked over to him and put her arm lightly around his neck.

"Norman, I've got a favor to ask you. Wait. Don't speak. Let me finish. If you think it over you'll see that I've got good reasons for asking you. From every point of view you're the ideal person."

He leaned forward and kissed her cheek.

"Suppose you tell me what you want," he said, smiling.

"I want you to let me appoint you Peter's legal guardian in the event of my death."

He was silent in amazement.

"Don't you see the advantages?" she continued. "You've got an official position. Peter likes you. And everyone will accept you as a family friend. We'll have an excuse to meet."

"It's an odd way of making a relationship respectable," he said.

"What's so odd about it?" she cried. "Far more sensible to appoint a promising young man in the Foreign Office than some stuffy old solicitor."

"I may be posted abroad at any moment."

"I'm hardly likely to die at any moment. At least, I hope not."

"Daphne, be reasonable . . ." he began.

But in the end he allowed himself to be persuaded.

During the next three months he seldom met her. Believing that she was being excessively cautious he telephoned several times, but there always seemed to be some reason why she could not meet him. He began to wonder whether Daphne had not discarded him now that he had finished his work on the play and it was a success. But early in the spring she telephoned and begged him to come down to Mullings for the weekend.

"Peter's back from school," she said, "and he's longing to see you and so am I. It's been ages since we met. You've neglected us both, you brute."

"I've only rung you a dozen times."

"You know that horror Muriel always forgets to give me messages."

He collected her at the theater on Saturday after the evening performance. They had supper in Soho and drove down in his car to Mullings afterward. Daphne was happy and affectionate. She behaved as if they had been seeing each other constantly, and Norman was delighted to be with her again. His work that week in the office had been exacting, and it was a relief to be with a companion whose interest in Europe was chiefly concerned with food, wine, and clothes.

Daphne slept late in the country, and as usual Norman had breakfast in his room the following morning. At ten he wandered downstairs and looked vaguely around for Peter. He felt a little guilty that he had not found time to go down to Eton during that spring. He discovered from Daphne's mottle-faced butler that Master Peter had gone out for a walk.

Norman strolled around the garden for a while and then went back indoors and settled himself with the Sunday newspapers in the long room that had been the courtyard of the house and was now used by Daphne as a drawing room. It was comfortably furnished with a gallery running around two sides of it.

At noon Daphne appeared in a new Paris dress looking as springlike as the daffodils, and a few minutes later Peter came in and greeted them both. Peter seemed unusually happy. He stood with his head thrown back gazing at each of them in turn. With his wide-set eyes and his uptilted nose and wide mouth he sometimes looked astonishingly like the photographs Norman had seen of Daphne playing Peter Pan. He was very slender, and though he had been out walking his face was pale. He had his mother's charm but none of her robust vitality.

"Well? Aren't you going to say anything to me?" he asked, after staring at them for a while.

"What do you want us to say?" Daphne asked, laughing.

"You're teasing me."

"No, we're not."

"You mean you really don't know what to say?"

"My dear child, what *are* you talking about?"

As she spoke the happiness left his face.

"You've forgotten what day it is."

"Good heavens!" Daphne cried. "It's the boy's birthday and I'd clean forgot. Why did no one remind me? I'm hopelessly vague about dates. My darling Peter, forgive your poor erring mother and come and give her a birthday kiss."

Peter did not move. He glared at her, white-faced and sullen.

"I did remind you," he blurted out.

"I don't believe it for one moment," Daphne said lightly.

"I told you when you were down last weekend."

"I'm sorry, my pet. But your mother's a hard-working woman these days."

"You might not have had time to get me a present, but at least you could have remembered."

Peter turned to Norman.

"So could you," he added.

"Darling, now you're just being silly," Daphne said, smiling brightly to disguise her annoyance. "Why on earth should Norman remember your birthday?"

"Because I'm his guardian," Norman said quietly. "Peter, I'm sorry."

"Because you asked me at the first night party," Peter corrected him. "And then I asked you when your birthday was and you said it was on the twenty-sixth of September. I haven't forgotten."

"Now you're being childish and rude," Daphne said. "And I thought I'd brought you up to have good manners."

"No one's remembered my birthday. No one in all the world."

"Darling, if you're going to be tiresome you'd better go upstairs to your room."

"That's just where I am going," Peter said.

Suddenly he burst into tears and ran up the flight of stairs that led from the hall to the gallery.

Daphne got up from her chair with a sigh and smoothed down her dress.

"What a fuss about nothing!" she said. "I'm afraid he's at that awkward age. Let's have a gin and tonic. Be an angel and tell Cooper to bring in some ice."

16

The drums were still thudding relentlessly, the sound fading, then swelling as the tempo quickened. Norman got up and threw a log on the fire. The kerosene lamp had burned out from lack of fuel, and I could only see his face by the light of the leaping flames. He looked exhausted, but his voice had never faltered as he told me the first part of his story, and I had noticed that he had not touched the brandy since we had come back into the house.

While he continued his story I tried to forget the shabby
defeated man in the chair opposite me; I tried to imagine him
as he had been at thirty-eight, erect and confident, handsome
and glowing with charm.

Peter's bitter sobs haunted Norman for many days after the
weekend, and he determined to go down to Eton to visit him.

One Saturday morning early in May, Norman found himself in London with nothing to do. He telephoned Daphne
and told her that he could drive down to Eton that afternoon.
Daphne was delighted.

"I can't get down because of your wretched play," she
said. "God! what a run! And last night we had the 'full house'
notices out again."

"Should I ring his housemaster?"

"Heavens no. You're his guardian, aren't you? Just wire
Peter that you're turning up. Give him all my love, won't you?"

At four o'clock that afternoon Norman walked into the
house where Peter boarded and discovered that his wire had
arrived too late. Peter had gone out. He learned from a boy
he met outside Peter's dark little room that Peter was on the
river.

"You'll find him easily enough. He never goes far," the boy
said scornfully.

As Norman wandered down Keates Lane, across the
meadows toward the towpath, he was assailed by memories
far sadder and more poignant than he had thought possible.
He could no longer remember the fears and humiliations of
his first year as a lower boy at Eton – the bleak classrooms, the
cold mud of the playing fields in the damp gray afternoons;
he could only recall other days when the school buildings had
seemed empty and asleep in the sunshine and he had strolled
across the fields with a friend to bathe at Cuckoo Weir; he
could smell the warm grass; he could feel the rough towel
tucked under his arm and the shock when he dived in and the
water engulfed his hot body. He could even remember the
name of his friend. It was Hemming, and he had a mole on

his right shoulder. Norman had seldom thought about him for twenty years.

Norman sat down on the bank by the towpath and watched the boats glide by. He felt at peace with the world. The problems he had left behind on his desk had lost their importance. Suddenly his heart leaped with pleasure as he recognized Peter sculling downstream toward him. He was rowing smoothly and neatly but without effort, as if the movement were more important than the speed.

"Ahoy! Peter!" Norman shouted.

Peter rested on his oars and turned around. When he saw Norman his solemn face was lit by a smile of joy.

"Norman!" he cried out, and then blushed.

By the time he reached Norman the serious withdrawn look had come back into his face.

"I'll meet you at the boathouse," Norman said. "Then we'll go to the Cockpit for tea if you've nothing better to do."

"Fine."

Norman watched him row back to the boathouse. Though Peter looked very slender in his singlet and shorts, his shoulders were quite broad and his chest was deep.

Tea was a success. There was no need for Peter to talk because he was absorbed in the business of eating. Enviously Norman saw him finish three plates of scones with strawberry jam and Devonshire cream. But afterward, while they strolled along the High Street Norman tried in vain to get the boy to talk. Peter was nervous and constrained, and Norman had the impression that he was longing to get back to his friends. They stopped beside Norman's car.

"Have you got to go back?" Peter blurted out unexpectedly. "There's plenty of time left."

"Sorry, but I must be in London in time to change for dinner."

"What about next Saturday then?"

Norman looked at him in surprise. Then he realized he had made no mistake about the pleading note in the voice. Peter's wide blue eyes were watching him anxiously.

"I won't promise," Norman said. "But I'll do my best."

"Please do."

Norman went down to Eton the following Saturday and the next. By now he had realized that for some reason Peter was deeply unhappy. Not only was he fond of the boy and sorry for him, but he had become interested in the character that was hidden by the layers of reserve. Why was the boy so unhappy? Though Peter was obviously fond of his company, Norman could not find out. Peter shied away from his questions like a colt.

After their third afternoon together Norman decided that he was the wrong person to deal with the boy's problems. He would discuss the matter with Daphne when they next met. If Daphne refused to help, then at least she must have a talk with Peter's housemaster.

"Incidentally, Peter, I can't get down next Saturday," he said as he got into his car.

"That doesn't matter because the Monday after that is the Fourth of June, and you must come down for that. Mummy's coming too. Surely you can get away from your boring old office for the Fourth of June?"

"I'm not so sure," Norman said, smiling.

On the morning of the fourth Daphne telephoned Norman from Kent.

"Darling, I've waked up with the most cracking headache," she said. "I just can't face Eton today. All those stuffy women in floppy clothes staring at me. And I look a perfect wreck. I must get some rest if I'm to face the evening performance. Vivian can't get away. I've just phoned him. Please be an angel and go yourself."

Norman had not intended to leave London that Monday. He looked at the mass of papers in his in-tray. Then he saw Peter's worried face.

"All right," he said. "But I shan't be able to get down till after lunch."

"Bless you. Thank heavens I've got one kind friend."

"Daphne, can you lunch with me this week? There's something I have to discuss with you."

"Is it a new play? Darling, how thrilling!"

"No. It's about Peter."

"Of course we must talk about Peter. Any day you say, but not this week. Darling, give me a ring a week today. Will you?"

"Hold on a moment, Daphne. What time did Peter expect you?"

"Toward noon. But don't fuss. If I ring him now I'll be sure to catch him. Bless you. Good-bye."

Norman had an early lunch and drove down to Eton without bothering to change out of his gray flannel suit. He found Peter waiting outside his house.

"It was good of you to come," Peter cried. He was looking very smart. His top hat had been newly blocked, and a pink carnation sprouted from the buttonhole of his freshly pressed tail suit.

"Shall we stroll up to Agar's Plough?" Norman asked.

"If you want to."

"Isn't one supposed to watch the cricket on the Fourth of June?" Norman asked, laughing.

"I suppose so."

It was a warm, dry day, and hosts of friends and relations and Old Etonians were swarming slowly around the playing field. Norman met several people he liked and several people he had avoided for years. He noticed, however, that Peter had not found any friends to greet in the crowd. Toward teatime Peter's silence began to disturb him.

"What's the trouble?" Norman asked bluntly.

"It's awfully hot in these clothes," Peter muttered.

"What about an ice in the shade?"

Peter turned around and faced him.

"Do you want to stay here?" he asked.

"Not particularly," Norman answered in surprise. "What else is there to do?"

"We could go for a swim."

"Is that what you'd like?"

"Not if you don't want to."

"Where could we go?"

"Anywhere, so long as none of the others would be there."

"What about absence?"

"As soon as I heard that you were coming and Mummy wasn't I asked my tutor for leave. I hoped you wouldn't mind going for a swim."

"All right. Any particular place you'd like to go?"

"No. But the further away the better."

As they walked back toward the college Norman remembered a quiet reach of the Thames near Wargrave.

"Come in and talk to me while I change," Peter said. "I can't go out swimming in these clothes."

Norman had never known him so eager and cheerful. Peter rushed to the chest in his small room and flung out the clothes he needed. Then he ripped off his tail coat and waistcoat and struggled to undo his stiff collar as if each second were valuable. When he pulled off his shirt and striped trousers Norman was half shocked and half amused to see that he wore no underclothes. Peter dressed in frenzied haste, snatched up a towel and some bathing trunks, and turned to Norman.

"Let's go!" he said, laughing. "What are you waiting for?"

During the drive to Wargrave Peter chattered away happily. But Norman noticed that it was always the holidays he talked about – never school.

Norman left his car in a shady lane, took an old bathing suit out of the back of the trunk, and led the way across a meadow to the place he remembered. To Peter's joy it was deserted.

"The bank's a bit muddy, but it's all right when you're in," Norman said.

"Just watch," Peter laughed.

He stood ten yards away from the bank, took a running jump, and landed well away from the rushes. In the water he seemed to become a different person. He swam with quick clean strokes for a while. Then he rolled and twisted and dived under and came up on the opposite side, choking and laughing. As he stood on the far bank waving to Norman, who was swimming upstream, his lithe body looked wonderfully graceful.

For an hour his whole being seemed transformed. He was radiantly happy. But when he got out of the water, panting with exhaustion, and lay on the bank drying in the sun he became solemn again. He answered Norman's questions briefly, almost sullenly. Norman wondered at his change of mood. Then he thought of a reason for it.

"What a fool I am!" Norman exclaimed. "We ought to have brought a friend of yours along with us."

Peter did not move. He was leaning on his elbow gazing at the river.

"I've got no friend to bring," he said.

"Nonsense," Norman said gently.

"I haven't. Not one."

"That can't be true."

"It is, though."

"There must be someone in your house?"

"In my house? I hate the whole lot of them," Peter said quietly. "I hate them."

Suddenly, he buried his face in the grass and began to cry with long racking sobs.

When Norman tried to comfort him the boy's sobbing became more convulsive. His body was shaking with the intensity of his grief, his hands were clasped tightly over his face to suppress the sound of his weeping. Norman waited in silence. A lark was wheeling in the blue sky, and the sun was slanting through the willows. Presently the sobbing ceased. But now and then the boy's chest would heave in a shuddering sigh.

"Suppose you tell me what it's all about?" Norman said gently.

Peter took his hands away from his face and raised his head and looked up at Norman.

"I know what it can be like," Norman said.

Then, at last, the walls of Peter's reticence were broken, and the words came pouring out in a passionate stream.

Norman soon realized that his case was not unusual. Peter had not been sent to a preparatory school because he was delicate. He had been brought up first by a governess and then by a tutor. When he went to Eton it was the first time he had left home and it was the first time he had mixed with boys of his own age. He was nervous and shy. The boys in his house mistook his reticence for conceit. From the first week he was unpopular. He had not learned to attune his opinions with those of the mob. When he was shocked by their dirty stories, they considered him an opinionated prig. When he was frightened and revolted by their horseplay they thought he was effeminate. His milk-and-white complexion and slender build invited bullying. For his first year as a lower boy he had been wretched. The bullying had been stopped now. He could sit alone in his room and read without fear of the tramping feet in the passage outside. But he was still the unpopular boy of the house, the outcast.

"I've still not got a single friend," Peter said. "I know it's all my own fault. But I do try to be like them. Really I do."

Peter rolled over onto his back and stared up at the sky.

"Shall I tell you something?" Peter said. "You're the only person who cares tuppence about me. You're the only person in all the world."

"What nonsense! To start with, your mother's devoted to you."

"Mummy!" Peter cried. "She doesn't care. She hasn't been down once to see me this half."

"That's because she's acting every single day of the week in my play. And she needs to rest on Sunday."

"She's just plain bored with me."

"You mustn't say that. It's not true. Your mother loves you, and you know it," Norman said, forcing the note of conviction into his voice.

"I knew she wouldn't come down today. And shall I tell

you something else? As soon as I heard you were coming I wasn't a bit sorry."

"I won't let you speak like that about your mother. It's stupid and ungrateful. I know that she's terribly fond of you. And you should have told her every word about your house that you've told me. You see, Peter, there's nothing so very unusual about it. Thousands of people have been in your position before. Thousands will be in it again. . . ."

Gazing straight ahead at the river shining in the evening sun, Norman began to speak of the lonely people in the world, the misjudged, the outsiders. Gently he urged the need to make some compromise to fit in with the people around one, while remaining intact in oneself. He could now speak sincerely, for he had felt himself a misfit until he went to Oxford and discovered the security and happiness of being one of a crowd. He told Peter of his own fears and blunders during his first years at Eton. And as he spoke he was back once again in the old red building. Outside he could hear the feet scudding on the pavement. He was late for the early school, and they had stolen his only tie. He rushed into the room next door and pulled open the drawers. The school clock was striking. There was no hope now. He would arrive late in school. And next time, the master had said – next time . . . He knew it would mean a beating. Frantically, he rushed into another room. . . . As he remembered his panic, Norman realized that nothing in the war had frightened him so much. Life, he told Peter, had never faced him since with such stark overwhelming terror. As a boy he had lacked a sense of proportion; he had been oversensitive. If only his father and mother had been alive, if only there had been someone to explain that his misery would not last, that he must not turn in on himself but make every effort to break down the barriers that kept him from friendship, he might have been happier at school. At least he would not have known the bitter misery of feeling all alone in a careless world.

Peter was silent when he had finished. Norman turned away from the river to look at him. Peter was lying on one arm staring down at the grass, his head averted.

"What is it, Peter?" Norman asked softly.

"Nothing."

"Look at me."

Unwillingly Peter turned his head. His lips were trembling, and tears were slowly running down his cheeks.

"What's wrong?"

"It's all right," Peter said. "Really it is. I'm silly, I know I am. But it's like going home for the holidays. Except it's better because this time I know it'll never matter again so much."

Norman felt a sense of deep relief. At least when Peter most needed him he had not failed.

Then, while he looked at the boy's tear-stained face turned up to him in gratitude, Norman felt his heart contract, as if a hand were grasping it gently. He felt faint and closed his eyes. But he could still see the tear-stained face. And at that moment, with a start of horror, Norman recognized the emotion that overwhelmed him – a hopeless tenderness mixed with anguish that he had not felt for more than twenty years but which had now returned from the past, stronger and deeper than before. With an awful certainty Norman knew that he loved Peter.

At last he acknowledged to himself the truth he had cunningly withheld for so long. The shock numbed him. He did not know for how long he remained motionless. When he opened his eyes Peter was watching him inquiringly.

Norman turned away violently from the slender body sprawling on the grass beside him. He reached over for his coat and took out his wrist watch from the pocket.

"We must go," he said harshly. "It's late."

"But there must be plenty of time yet," Peter said in surprise.

"I must get back to London. Hurry up and dress. I'm late as it is."

They drove back to Eton in silence. Norman could not trust his voice not to betray the emotion that seared his heart. When the school buildings came into sight Peter spoke.

"You're not cross with me, are you?" he asked. "Because I was stupid, I mean."

"No, Peter. I'm not cross with you."

"When will you come down next?"

"I don't know. I have to go to Paris for a conference," Norman said truthfully.

"But you'll be back for Lord's?"

"Perhaps not."

"Promise you'll come down at least once more this half."

"I'll try to. But I can't promise."

"If you promise, then I'll promise I'll do all I can to make friends."

"Very well," Norman said. "I'll come down once more."


17


Norman stretched out his hand and took a cigarette from the box on the table. I got up and gave him a light. He pointed questioningly toward the whisky on the sideboard, but I shook my head.

"That night I spent the evening alone in my flat," Norman continued. "I won't weary you with my wretched, confused thoughts. I can never explain to you how appalled I was. Not that I was an innocent. I wasn't. Few people who have spent four years in a boarding school can be. When I was sixteen I had felt the pangs of adolescent love for a boy a little younger than myself. A year later it was almost forgotten. And when I went to Oxford I only thought of it as an inevitable part of the school days I had put firmly behind me. I went after girls like the rest of our crowd.

"But that evening I knew why, for all my affairs, I had never fallen in love.

"Toward dawn I forced myself to make various decisions. The first, obviously, was that I must never let Peter guess my feelings. I must be constantly on guard. Secondly, for my own sake, I must see him as seldom as possible. But the boy was

lonely and needed sympathy. Therefore, lastly, I must persuade Daphne to take more interest in him.

"On Tuesday morning I telephoned Daphne and we arranged to have supper after the evening performance on
Friday. What strange details the memory retains! I can remember that when I put down the receiver it was damp
from my hand. On Tuesday evening I had a letter from Peter
thanking me for taking him out. 'I've reckoned the days,' he
ended, 'and if you don't come down till after Lord's I shan't
see you for nearly six weeks. Can't you come down just once
before then?'

"The next morning as I walked to the office I was passing a jeweler's shop when I remembered that I had never
given Peter a birthday present. I stopped and looked in at the
window. I knew that Peter did not have a wrist watch. There
were several displayed in the window, but they were set in
gold. However, I walked in and chose the plainest of them
and sent it to Peter with a note saying that I could not come
down to Eton until the Saturday after the Eton and Harrow
match.

"On Friday night I took Daphne to supper at the quiet restaurant she liked in Soho. The whole evening was a ghastly
failure."

From the very start of the evening Daphne had been in a
bad temper. During the last fortnight of warm weather, at-
tendance had dropped at the theater, and Cole Edwards was
thinking of taking off the play. For the first time Daphne
blamed Norman for not making the alteration she had
wanted in the last act.

"The whole play drops at that moment," she said, "and
there's nothing I can do about it. If only you'd listened to
me."

Norman tried to calm her down as best he could and presently began to speak about Peter.

"Darling, aren't you rather overdoing your guardian
stunt?" Daphne asked him suddenly.

"What do you mean?"

"You must know the boy's got a mad crush on you."

Norman felt a stab of guilt. "What makes you think so?" he asked, laughing.

"For one thing, his voice when I phoned to say that I couldn't come down to the Fourth of June."

"He was terribly disappointed."

"Until he found out you were coming, then he didn't even trouble to disguise his pleasure."

"Daphne, you're exaggerating wildly. Of course he wanted someone to come down to take him out."

"I still think you're spoiling him. You've been down there almost every Saturday this half, so I'm told. Isn't that rather overdoing it? You must be careful. You know how people gossip. And you know that he's wildly emotional."

Though Daphne spoke lightly, Norman detected an undercurrent of hostility in her voice. He decided to ignore her obvious hint.

"The boy's lonely. That's what I wanted to talk to you about," he said.

"Rot. He's got plenty of friends."

"But he hasn't. That's just the point."

"My dear, I know my own son. He'll settle down in time if he's left alone. He's got to learn that life isn't all a bed of roses."

Daphne leaned across the table and touched his hand.

"Norman, don't let's quarrel," she said with an affection-ate smile. "We're such good friends. Besides, I want you to write another play for me," she added, laughing.

The following morning Norman received a wild letter of gratitude from Peter. "Don't forget the Saturday after Lord's," the letter ended. That afternoon Norman left for Paris.

While abroad Norman decided that he would indeed go down to visit Peter again, but it would be for the last time. Though he did not believe what Daphne had said, he realized the danger. Peter was starved of affection; he might easily become overdevoted to anyone who was kind to him. There-fore, tactfully but firmly Norman must withdraw from his life. Later, perhaps . . . But he would not let himself contemplate the future.

On the appointed Saturday Norman found Peter waiting outside his house at three o'clock. The sun was burning down from a hot white sky.

"Look!" Peter said, pulling up his sleeve to display the wrist watch.

"It looks quite smart. What would you like to do this afternoon? Shall we go round the Castle?"

Peter's face fell.

"It's awfully muggy in the town," he said. "And I've got leave."

"Where shall we go, then? What about Henley?"

"Can't we go back to that place for a swim? Please say yes."

"Very well."

"I've kept my side of the promise," Peter said as they drove toward Wargrave. "I've tried really hard. And there's one boy I've made great friends with."

Norman was dismayed to feel a throb of jealousy.

"What's he like?" he asked lightly.

"He's a year older than me and terrifically good at games. I'm going to ask Mummy if I can ask him to stay next holidays. You'll come down too, won't you?"

"I'm not sure. I've a mass of work and my weekends are booked up for a long time ahead."

"Promise to come down once."

"You don't catch me as easily as that a second time," Norman said, laughing.

Once again they lay on the bank drying in the hot sun.

"What are you thinking about?" Peter asked.

"I was wondering why this meadow was always deserted," Norman lied.

"Why is it?"

"Though the gate's open at the far end, it may be private property. We're probably trespassing."

"Then if anyone comes we'll have to pick up our clothes and run for it. And I bet you can run fast. You're jolly lean for your age."

"In a few years' time I'll be a scraggy old man."

"Bollocks."

Norman laughed.

"You'd better not use that language at home," he said.

Norman was determined to be briskly cheerful throughout the afternoon. Never must he allow the conversation to grow serious. But though he tried hard to amuse Peter he found his phrases languished in the oppressive heat, and Peter was oddly silent.

"What about another swim?" Norman suggested.

"Let's wait awhile."

Norman looked up at the sun.

"There's not much more time if you want some tea," he said.

Peter turned onto his side and stared at him.

"What's up?" Peter asked abruptly.

"Nothing."

"You're worried about something. Have I done anything wrong?"

"Heavens no!"

"You're not cross?"

"Why should I be, you idiot?" Norman laughed.

"That's all right then. But you look tired. Why don't you doze for a while?"

"That's not a bad idea."

Norman leaned back against the pillow of his coat. For a while he gazed up at the sky, his mind beating against the waves of sadness that washed over him. Presently he closed his eyes. But he was so intensely aware of the boy lying beside him that he heard the rustle of grass caused by the slight movement toward him. Then Peter took hold of his hand and gently drew it toward him.

At that instant, Norman knew that Peter shared his emotions. They had reached the frontier of a land from which there could be no safe return. While his heart rocked, Norman made his decision.

For a few seconds Norman let his hand lie still. Then, slowly, casually, he withdrew it.

"If I smoke a cigarette it'll keep the flies away," he said in a clear steady voice.

"Don't you want to sleep?"

"Not nearly as much as I want a cigarette," Norman said, taking his case and lighter out of his coat pocket.

Peter was looking up at him with wide, inquiring eyes.

"Do you know the old definition of a cigarette?" Norman asked lightly.

"No."

"Smoke at one end and a fool at the other."

"That's not bad."

The moment of danger was passing. If he could keep talking now without faltering it might pass for ever.

"I tell you what, Peter. If you promise not to touch a cigarette until you're twenty-one I'll give you— What would you like? Tell me."

"When I'm twenty-one? I can't think. It's so far off."

"You'll be surprised how quickly the day will come."

"Promise you'll be at my party."

"Certainly. And I shall give you a long moral lecture that'll bore you to distraction."

"How do you know it will?"

"Because I've heard it several times before."

Peter laughed.

"I'm going in for a last swim," he said, scrambling to his feet. "Come on, lazy."

The moment had passed.

The next morning Daphne telephoned to tell Norman that the play was being taken off the following week.

"After all, we've had a long run," she concluded.

"Entirely thanks to you."

"Nonsense. Cole Edwards told me to ask you if you've got another play on the stocks."

"No. This one was only a flash in the pan."

"I don't believe it. You must write another."

"By the way, I saw Peter yesterday."

"Did you?"

Daphne was a good actress, but Norman felt that her casual tone was forced.

"He's far happier."

"I'm so glad," Daphne said quickly. "That reminds me, Norman. I particularly want you to come down to Mullings the first weekend in August. Cole will be there and the Rossiters. It's just your cup of tea – half stage, half political. Peter will be back from school, of course. You simply must come."

"Thanks awfully, but I can't," Norman replied truthfully. "There's a dreary official reception on Saturday evening that I daren't miss."

"What time does it start?"

"Six-thirty."

"What time will it be finished?"

"Nine, with any luck."

"Then you can drive down afterward. You know how late we stay up."

"Can't we make it a weekend in September?" Norman had heard that he might be sent to Rome at any moment.

"Why are you trying to get out of coming? Are you going to drop me the instant I've finished in your play?"

"I thought the boot was on the other foot."

"Well, it's not. And I won't hear another word of excuse. We'll expect you any time after eleven that Saturday. I'll have some cold food waiting for you."


That Saturday evening Norman managed to slip away from the reception at nine. He collected his suitcase from his flat and drove down to Kent. He felt tired and dispirited. At least Peter would have gone to bed by the time he arrived. He dreaded meeting the boy again, and yet he longed for the moment. But he would not have to face that ordeal until morning, and he looked forward to meeting Cole and Rossiter again. Though Rossiter was reputed to have a sharp tongue, Norman had found him witty and charming. He was a plump, sleek man of middle age with a drawling voice that seemed to add point to the wit of his remarks. He had married his rather dull wife for her money, but he behaved as if he were devoted to her. He was an adroit politician with considerable influence for his age. The Rossiters had taken up Daphne when she first came to London. They were Daphne's oldest friends.

When Norman turned down the drive to the house his fatigue left him. He began to feel pleasantly excited. It was only a quarter past eleven, and the lights of the drawing room shone out onto the wide sweep of gravel. He pulled the long bell handle outside the porch and waited in the warm, still night. The smell of sweetbrier floated up from the garden below the terrace. After some delay the parlormaid opened the front door. Perhaps it was Cooper's evening off.

"Good evening, sir."

"Good evening. Have the other guests arrived?"

"Yes, sir. They've been expecting you."

Norman walked quickly through the entrance hall and opened the door of the drawing room.

Daphne and her three guests were standing in silence in front of the empty, stone fireplace. They were staring up at the gallery that led from the top of the stairs at the far end of the room. Immediately, Norman sensed the tension. As he moved into the room they turned toward him. . . .

It was not until several months later that Norman learned from a friend of Cole Edwards what had happened in that room before he arrived.

When Cooper had brought in the coffee after dinner, Daphne had reminded him that Norman was expected some time after eleven.

"Let me know when you see the lights of Mr. Hartleigh's car coming down the drive," Daphne said. "And ask Muriel to stay up. I may need her later."

"Certainly, madam."

At a quarter past eleven Cooper came back into the room.

"There's the lights of a car coming down the drive now, madam," he announced.

Daphne moved toward him.

"Go up and wake Master Peter," she said. "Tell him I want to speak to him at once. Be quick. It's urgent."

Cooper hurried up the stairs and disappeared along the gallery. A few moments later he returned.

"Master Peter will be here in a minute," he said.

"Thank you, Cooper. That will do."

Cooper walked down the stairs and went out of the door that led to the dining room. No one spoke. The three guests already knew what Daphne intended to do, and they had tried to dissuade her in vain. It was a plan that only an actress could have conceived. Up to the last moment Cole had been unable to believe that she would really go ahead with it.

Then Peter appeared. He had put on a dressing gown over his pajamas. His hair was tousled, and he was half-dazed with sleep. He leaned over the side of the gallery, blinking down at them.

"What is it, Mummy?" he asked.

"Peter, I'm afraid I've got some awfully bad news," Daphne said slowly, her eyes fixed on the boy's pale face. "Norman has accepted an appointment as counselor to our embassy in Tokyo. He's leaving England tomorrow, and he'll be away for six years."

Peter gazed down at her, half-stricken, half-disbelieving.

At that moment Norman walked into the room. He looked slender and distinguished in the clothes he had worn for the reception. For an instant he stood perfectly serene and erect, watching the group by the fireplace. But when they turned toward him in silence, the smile left his face, and he stared at them in bewilderment.

Then, with a desperate cry, Peter ran the length of the gallery and rushed down the stairs.

Rigid with consternation Norman watched the boy leap into the hall and turn toward him.

When Peter saw the lines of Norman's face set in a hard expression as never before, he began to sob. Blindly he stumbled across the room and threw himself into Norman's arms.

"Tell me it's not true," he cried. "Tell me it's not true."

Daphne's harsh voice pierced the sound of the boy's hysterical sobbing.

"Now get out, Norman," she said. "We'll send your gold watch after you. Get out, and leave the boy alone."

## 18

The drums had stopped, and the room seemed very quiet. Intermittently, I could see Norman's face lit by a tiny flame that still flickered.

"Daphne followed me out into the hall," he continued in a flat, expressionless voice. "She said more, shouting down my protestations – but I was too broken and dazed to remember. Later, she told her friends that her motive for causing the scene was to break my hold on Peter once and for all. I don't believe it. I realize now that during those early months of rewriting and rehearsing the play I had wounded her vanity by not making love to her. Then, with Peter, I had made her doubly jealous. She wanted to get even with me. Perhaps the motives were confused in her tortuous mind.

"The fact remains. She planned that scene a fortnight ahead, and it succeeded brilliantly. That night I drove back to London and sent in my resignation from the Foreign Office."

"But why, for heaven's sake?" I asked. "You weren't guilty."

"Not in law. No. But I knew Daphne's guests well enough to realize that gossip would spread. And I knew London well enough to appreciate that no threat of an action for slander could stop it. But there was a far stronger reason than that.

The whole smug edifice of self-esteem and morality that I had built up for myself had been shattered when Peter ran into my arms. I knew which side of the fence I was on. And it was the wrong side.

"I settled my affairs and left England a month later. I've never been back since."

I leaned forward to ask a question and then decided against it. Furtively I settled back into my chair. But Norman had seen my head move.

"I think I know the question you were going to ask," he said. "The answer is that he died of meningitis when he was eighteen. And with him died the hope that I'd nurtured for two years, the hope that one day we'd meet again and it would be all right."

Norman slowly raised himself from his chair and walked across to a table and picked up a flashlight.

"I'll show you his photograph," he said.

He took a key out of his pocket and unlocked the top drawer of the desk. By the light of the flashlight I could see him fumbling through packets of letters and documents. At last he produced an unframed photograph mounted on cardboard. He handed it to me together with the light.

"It was taken just after that Fourth of June," Norman said.

I stared at the photograph in amazement.

The stiffly curling hair, the rather worried eyes, the delicate nostrils and small fleshy nose, the wide mouth – the resemblance was fantastic. It was Bill Wayne gazing at me from the cardboard; Bill eight years younger. I wondered whether Norman had taken out the wrong photograph. But printed at the bottom of the cardboard was the name and address of the photographer in Windsor, and at the right-hand corner in faded ink were written the words: "To Norman with love from Peter."

"The likeness is staggering, isn't it?" Norman said quietly.

"Were they related in some way?"

"No."

"Then the resemblance is pure chance?"

Norman sighed.

"Yes. In a way," he said.

The gossip followed Norman abroad. Moving through the interlocking circles of cosmopolitan society inaccurate rumors seeped into the cafés and bars and villas he frequented in Europe. From sly remarks and casual hints, sometimes from more direct approaches, Norman knew the reason given for his retirement. And as the months passed by he discovered that without any volition on his part he had been accepted by the crowd that drifted hopefully between a dozen fixed resorts. The scandal was his subscription fee, his proposer and seconder, all in one. He had been elected to the fraternity he had once despised. His coldness was attributed to shyness, his evasions to timidity.

At first, Norman resented the tacit understanding that he met. But gradually he found that the individuals varied in character, as in any other community. He made friends who sympathized not only with his emotions, but with his reserve. For a time Norman was happy in Europe. He had rented a villa outside Florence and he was writing another play. But the spontaneous wit, the lightness of touch, that had distinguished his efforts as an amateur, deserted him now that he was striving to be a professional. When half a dozen London managers had turned down his second play Norman left his villa and his newfound friends and sailed from Naples to the Near East, where he wrote his first book of travel. The book gained him little money but established him as a writer.

During the years before World War II Norman's private income was sufficient to allow him to travel where he pleased so long as he lived modestly. And he had now learned to avoid the towns, for only in the deserts and wild places could he find peace.

At the outbreak of war he was in the Sudan. He made his way to Cairo and reported to general headquarters. His knowledge of languages and his political training were valuable. He was immediately given a job in Intelligence. Norman was surprised to discover how glad he was to be in harness again. He worked behind the enemy lines, first in Abyssinia and later in the Balkans where he was made head of a particular organization for sabotage.

"In those days they weren't fussy about quirks of character," Norman said. "And the tainted wethers often led their flocks."

Though he spoke lightly about his work, I suspected that it was the strain of his various missions during those war years that made him now seem so much older than he was.

When the war ended Norman joined an Allied organization in Italy that dealt with the problem of refugees. During the autumn of 1946 he was living in Rome.

One Saturday evening in Rome, after an unusually exhausting week, Norman determined to go out and enjoy himself. He went first to a bar he had heard about in a street off the Via Bocca di Leone. It was an ordinary wineshop that was beginning to become well known. In a fortnight it would be crowded; within two months it would probably be closed by the police.

Norman sat down at an empty table by the door and ordered a fiaschino of Frascati wine. At the far end of the dingy room half a dozen young Italians were clustered around a guitar player. A few sailors and film extras leaned against the marble-topped bar. Their eyes slid toward Norman and rested on him without expression; then, when he gave no sign, their eyes shifted back to the counter.

Suddenly the door of the bar was flung open, and a young man walked in and stood irresolutely on the threshold, looking around the room as if uncertain whether to enter. He was wearing a worn pair of flannel trousers and a dirty brown jacket buttoned across a ragged singlet. But at that moment Norman did not notice the details of clothing, the frayed cuffs and cracked shoes; his gaze was fixed on the pale face and the blue, troubled eyes, on the straw-colored hair tumbling over a broad forehead; he was forcing himself to remember that Peter had died fifteen years ago – that this was a stranger.

The young man saw Norman staring at him and moved nervously toward his table.

"Mind if I sit down?" he asked in a rather pleasant Cockney voice.

"Please do. Cigarette?"

"Thanks."

"Are you working in Rome?"

"What's that got to do with you?"

The voice was now truculent. Norman smiled.

"Nothing – if you don't want to tell me."

The young man looked at him suspiciously, the cigarette twisting between his fingers.

"Then why did you ask me?" he muttered.

Norman ignored his question and called to the waiter to bring another glass.

"Like some wine?" he asked.

"All right."

"Can I ask how old you are? Or is that another desperate secret?"

For the first time Norman saw him smile, and memories of Peter surged across his mind.

"I'm twenty-three."

Norman poured out two glasses of wine. His hands were trembling. He felt lightheaded and reckless. The future no longer oppressed him. The dark mist had lifted, and for an instant he had seen a glimpse of his life as it might be yet. What words he now spoke across the little table did not much matter, for he sensed that though the young man had at some time been hurt badly his instincts were acutely enough developed to recognize a friend.

"Another dangerously secret question," Norman said. "When did you last have a square meal?"

"This morning."

"Square? With four courses?"

"All right. You win. Not for three days."

"And that was how I met Bill," Norman concluded.

He had put the photograph back in the drawer and settled down in the armchair again.

"But why was Bill in Rome of all places?"

"He'd left England because he'd been in trouble."

"What kind of trouble?"

"You must ask Bill that question. I don't suppose he minds so much talking about it now. But it took me a long time to find out. Suspicion of any type of official was deeply ingrained in him by then. He'd had a bad spell, and I knew it would take him some time to get over it. He wanted to start afresh in some place where there was a future for him.

"His mother's family had been farmers. He'd always loved the holidays he spent with them on the farm. Tanganyika seemed the ideal place."

"And is it – for you, I mean?"

Norman watched the little flame leaping between the two charred logs.

"Almost," he said quietly. "During the last three years I've been as happy as I can ever expect to be."

Norman threw the end of his cigarette into the fire.

"Every morning that he's here," he continued, "I stand on the terrace and watch him striding away across the garden which he never notices, crossing the open stretch of grass beyond, leaping the irrigation ditch, disappearing below the horizon into the maize plantations near the swamp, his head thrust forward slightly as if more eager than his body. I see, last of all, his shirt like a white bird fluttering in the distance. And the rest of my day's not empty because I know he's well and happy."

The pale light of dawn was filtering through the curtains. The air was heavy with smoke. I walked across and opened the French windows that led onto the veranda, and looked out. Thick banks of mist were rising from the swamp. I stepped out and stood watching the mist covering the vast landscape with a fleecy cloak while Norman's voice came softly from the smoky room.

"Here I am with Bill – for better or for worse. The farm's

losing money, and I've invested nearly all my capital in it. The money from your film would have been very useful. But I expect you can see now why I don't want that film made."

A deep red sun was rising out of the mist, and the birds were singing. I no longer felt tired; I had reached that state beyond exhaustion when the nerves overcome the body's need for rest. I could smell the earth and the grass, all fresh from the rain. Then some movement inside the room made me turn around.

In the half light I saw the door from the passage open and the young native girl creep in silently on her bare feet. For an instant she looked about, as if to make certain that Norman was alone before moving toward him. She was naked except for a red silk scarf tied round her loins. Her smooth skin gleamed like ebony. Norman was sitting with his eyes closed, his head drooping onto his chest, lost in his dreams. Gently the girl took the glass from his hand and put it on the table. Then she leaned over and kissed him on the forehead and took his hand and drew it to her breast, murmuring soft words I could not understand.

When Norman remained motionless she must have guessed that he was not alone, for she swung around suddenly and saw me standing on the veranda. With a little cry she sprang away from him and rushed out of the room.

Norman looked up and saw my eyes fixed on him, and once again he must have read my thoughts.

"Can't you understand?" he asked quietly. "The other thing lies mainly in the province of the mind."

In the silence we heard the sound of a truck rattling down the drive. We waited without speaking as it came to rest. Then Bill sprang onto the veranda, brushed past me with a quick apologetic smile, and ran into the room to Norman.

"God, I'm sorry!" he said. "Please forgive me."

"You deserve . . . No, I won't tell you what you deserve," Norman said grimly, without turning. "I'll wait until tomorrow."

But when Norman looked up at Bill's worried face he smiled.

"As for today," he said, "a very happy Christmas to you."

Suddenly Bill's eyes filled with tears.

"I should have said that first. And I've had my present for you in my pocket all the evening," he muttered, handing Norman a small box wrapped in paper. "I didn't buy it with money from the farm account either. It's my own money that I made from playing liar dice."

Bill turned to me while Norman opened the parcel.

"When I try to get him to write, he says he's got no pen. Well, this is a new type of fountain pen that can write ten thousand words at a stretch."

"Heaven forbid!" Norman murmured.

"Course you don't *have* to write that much," Bill grinned. He was happier now.

Norman examined the pen carefully.

"It's a beautiful present," he said, levering himself out of his chair. "I'm extremely grateful to you, Bill. And now you must both excuse me. You see before you an exhausted sodden old gentleman who's tottering to bed. Bill, shout for Luku to make you both bacon and eggs. That's what we ate when we'd stayed up all night in my young days."

"What about it?" Bill asked.

"Not for me," I said. "But I'd love some coffee before I go. I don't want to fall asleep at the wheel."

"Why don't you sleep here? There's a whole spare wing."

"No, thanks. I have a homing instinct."

"I'll shout for Luku to make some coffee, then."

Bill ran out onto the veranda and turned away toward the boys' quarters.

Norman was still standing by the door, watching me.

"Thank you for bearing with me," he said, and walked out of the room.

## 19

Bill and I sat on the veranda drinking black coffee that Bill had insisted on lacing with brandy.

"After all, it's not Christmas morning every day of the year."

The mist was drifting slowly away from the light green plain and the sun was beginning to warm the crisp air.

"Where on earth did you get to last night at the club?" I asked.

Bill frowned.

"I was a bloody fool. But Mary and I wanted to be somewhere alone together so we walked around to the guest-room block. There was no one about, of course. The door of one of the rooms was open and I looked in. The room was empty. No clothes, no suitcases – nothing. But there were towels laid out, and the bed was made. Obviously someone had booked it and hadn't turned up. Well, that was it. No one had seen us leaving, and we thought no one would notice if we didn't stay away too long."

"You were away a good half-hour."

"I heard what happened from Tim Curry. Mary and Barry had gone by then. I was a thoughtless, selfish idiot. I ought never to have left Norman alone so long. I'm sorry, David. I'm afraid I let you in for a lot of trouble."

"Did Tim tell you what the District Officer said?"

"Yes, I got the warning."

"What are you going to do about it?"

Bill scowled into his coffee cup.

"Barry's got no proof. We'll not be rash again. And he'll never find the place where we meet."

"Don't be a crass idiot. You know perfectly well he could find out from one of the boys. Luku, for instance."

"Luku! He's the last person. All he could tell you is that I sometimes drive to Iringa."

"What about the girl?"

"Halima doesn't know a thing."

"She's wildly attractive."

"I can see it. But I'd never touch Halima."

"Why not?"

Bill grinned, and then blushed.

"I suppose I'm old-fashioned that way."

"One of the boys near the place you meet Mary could easily tell Barry."

"There are none for miles around. Africa's a big country."

"I'm beginning to think it's surprisingly small."

Bill poured me out some more coffee and splashed in some brandy before I could stop him.

"What would you do in my place?" he asked.

"I can't guess. But I can tell you what I advise you to do. Go away with her or leave her alone."

Bill's eyes were wide with astonishment.

"We can't go away together."

"Why not?"

"Plain cash for one thing. We've neither of us got a penny. Norman for another. He can be an old bastard at times, but I can't leave him after all he's done for me. You don't know the half of it. I was in a pretty bad way when I met him."

The last shred of mist was floating like a ragged scarf in the blue sky. I looked at the scene carefully – the wide plain sloping down to the lighter green of the swamp, the blue hills beyond rolling gently to the horizon beneath the high dome of sky. I tried to impress on my memory the breadth and vastness of it all, for it was unlikely that I would ever see it again. Before I left for dinner with Norman I had received a cable from Stonor ordering me back to London as soon as I returned from safari and had got Norman's final decision. My job in the Southern Highlands was over.

I would probably never meet Norman or Bill again. But I liked them in an odd way, perhaps because chance had led me beneath the surface of their lives. At last the silly vignettes I had made from them in my mind were beginning to form a single picture. But there was still one gap, a small part of the canvas that needed filling in, and Bill's last words had reminded me of it.

"Norman told me you were in a bad way," I said. "He didn't tell me why."

"He didn't tell you I'd been in the glasshouse?"

"No."

"Well, that was it."

Bill gazed vacantly across the valley, twirling the cigarette between his fingers.

"I deserved what I got – the first part of it. I cheeked an officer two months before I was due to be demobbed."

Suddenly Bill flung down his cigarette and ground it with his heel.

"It doesn't seem to matter so much now. Funny, isn't it? In a way it's something to be able to talk about it. And I don't expect I was the only one it happened to. You see, there was a drill sergeant at the detention barracks kept picking on me. I knew what he was after and I wasn't having any. But he kept on faulting me till he got me sent to the solitary confinement cell. Then he'd got me just where he wanted me. He gave me the works, and he knew how to do it without leaving a mark. I held out for three days. Then something broke in me, and I just let him have what he wanted."

I was horrified by the story, but not surprised, for I had heard other stories of the same kind before; and each time I had grown indignant and asked for proof, and when no proof was available because of the victim's fear of giving evidence, I had shrugged my shoulders and forgotten, as others had done. Neighbors of minor Belsens, we stroll through our parish streets, heedless of what goes on in our prison bar- racks because they are out of sight and we cannot hear the screams. I lit a cigarette and sighed. During the long night it had occurred to me that if we were less tolerant of cruelty and more tolerant of illicit love the world might be a happier place.

"When I met Norman in Rome I was going to the bad

as fast as I could go," Bill was saying. "I reckon he saved
me."

"At least you can talk about it now."

As I spoke all the weariness that my nerves had kept at
bay descended on me. Vaguely I can remember finishing the
coffee. Then my mind goes blank until the moment that I
was sitting in the driving seat of my car and Bill was saying
good-bye to me. I had not yet decided what day I would leave.
I hoped that Tim Curry might be able to drive with me as far
as Dodoma.

"We'll be seeing you before you go?"

"I hope so," I said. "Bless you, Bill. So long."

There was no one about when I clambered stiffly out of my
car at the Rest House. Even Shabete seemed to be sleeping. I
closed the curtains in my little room and undressed and went
to bed.

I could still hear the relentless thudding of the drums
pounding through my uneasy dreams.

20

That afternoon I was wakened by knocking at the door. I
looked at my watch. It was five o'clock. I had slept for eight
hours.

"Come in," I shouted. "Karibou."

To my surprise Ma Bolting walked in. Though she seemed
perfectly calm I could see from her face that something was
wrong.

"Sorry to burst in on you," she said, "but we're in a bit of a
flap. Could you fling on some clothes and join us at the bar?"

"What's the trouble?"

"Barry Leyton, mainly. Can I make you some coffee?"

"Please. I'll be with you in five minutes."

As I plunged my face into cold water I reflected grimly
that Soho Square would seem an oasis of tranquillity after life

at Aruna. Yet part of me welcomed the excitement and was pleased that they needed my help.

I found Susan Curry alone with Ma Bolting in the bar. She looked tired and nervous.

"Thank God you're here," she cried. "You can't imagine . . ."

"Drink your coffee while it's hot. Now, Susan, just tell him quietly what's happened," Ma Bolting interrupted placidly.

"Barry drove over to our place earlier this afternoon," Susan said, trying to control her voice. "He wanted to see Tim, but I didn't want him to because Tim's got a bad attack of malaria – the shivering had come on even before we left the dance last night. Then Barry said it was urgent, he must see Tim alone. He insisted on going into the bedroom. He was in there talking for twenty minutes. When he came out he was in a black rage. He scarcely said good-bye to me. He flung out of the house and jumped into his car and drove away. Of course I went straight back to find out what had happened.

"Tim was looking ghastly. I've never seen him so upset. At first I couldn't get anything out of him because from the start Barry had sworn him to secrecy. Then Tim decided that he must tell me because he couldn't get up from his bed to give the warning himself.

"You remember that Barry came over to see Tim when you were away on safari, and we couldn't imagine what he wanted? Well, I know now. He wanted Tim to be a witness. He still does. That was why he came over again this afternoon."

"A witness? I don't understand."

"Barry's found out where Mary and Bill meet. He wants Tim to be a witness that Barry was on his property at a certain hour of the evening – at the hour, in fact, that Barry intends to wait outside the place where they meet. Apparently it's some unused hut. He wants an alibi 'in case of accidents' – those were the words he used."

Ma Bolting turned slowly toward me.

"It's been done out here before," she said grimly.

"Of course Tim refused," Susan continued. "Tim did all he could to stop him, but it was no good."

"When does he want the alibi?"

"For tonight."

"But Bill will be with Norman at their house, Imunda, tonight."

"I'm not sure," Susan said. "You see, Mary and Barry were asked over for a Christmas dinner by some friends of theirs who live outside the district. They were going to stay the night with them. But after lunch Mary said she didn't feel up to a long drive and another party, so Barry said he'd go alone and come back tomorrow afternoon. Mary must think she's safe. In fact, Barry's gone to this hut of theirs."

"Then we must warn her."

"That's just the trouble," Ma Bolting said quietly. "I saw Mary Leyton's Ford pass by our gates an hour ago. Susan must have missed her by twenty minutes."

"Which way was she going?"

"Toward Imunda."

"You mean . . ."

"I mean, I think she's fallen into the trap."

"But it's hardly a trap if she just goes to call on Norman and Bill."

I still thought they were exaggerating the possible danger.

"No. But she won't stay there."

"She'll collect Bill?"

"You still don't get it," Ma Bolting said. "They won't drive anywhere together in daylight. Mary will tell Bill to be at their meeting place tonight."

"Where is the hut?"

"We hoped you might know. We're not certain."

I tried to think quickly. Bill had said there were no boys for miles around the place where they met. It might lie in the direction of the long valley, perhaps within twenty miles of the village.

I looked at my watch. It was nearly five-thirty. The sun did not set until seven-fifteen.

"If you don't think they'll meet till after sunset there's a chance that Bill hasn't yet left," I said.

"You're right," Susan replied. "In that case he'll have got Tim's message. Tim sent off a boy with a letter before I left."

"I've seen letters lying about there unopened for days."

"Tim marked the envelope 'urgent and immediate.'"

"How long will it take the boy to reach Imunda?"

"He'll go across country. I should say about half an hour. He should be there by now."

"Then all may be well."

"If Bill's still there, yes. But what if he's not?"

As Susan spoke I remembered the District Officer's words: "I may not arrive in time to stop it."

"Is it any good trying to get hold of Jack Prescott?"

"We thought of that one. But he's away on safari."

"Do you seriously think that Barry . . ."

"Yes," Ma Bolting interrupted. "I do. And I've been out here for thirty years. One thing Susan forgot to tell you. Barry's got one witness already, but he wouldn't tell Tim the name."

"He could never get away with it."

"Perhaps not. But he may think he can."

"What can we do?"

Instinctively we both turned to Ma Bolting.

"If Bill's left without getting Tim's message, there's only one hope," she said. "Go across to Imunda. Find out from Norman Hartleigh where the hut is, and get there before sunset. There's still time."

"But why should Norman know where they meet?"

As Ma Bolting looked at me her expression changed.

"Because he's concerned with it in just the same way as Barry," she said in a voice cold with contempt. "Because poor Bill can't keep a secret from that man for long. Don't worry. Mr. Hartleigh knows all right, and he'd tell you, David."

"Very well. I'll drive to Imunda."

"Have a drink on the house before you go?"

"Thanks. Keep it till I come back."

The sun was slanting across a clear blue sky. Susan walked with me to my car.

"I hope it's all a wild goose chase," she said.

"Pray heaven it is."

Suddenly she took my hand and pressed it.

"Tim knew you would help," she said. "But I wasn't too sure."

"Nor was I. But there it is."

"Good luck."

"It's not me he's trying to shoot."

"Good luck all the same."

"Give my love to Tim, and bless you both."

"Don't drive too fast," she called after me.

I felt a little guilty because I had misjudged Susan Curry. She was a tiresome woman in many ways, but she was honest and sensible. She could not help being plain and dull. I began to feel rather sorry for her. I began to feel rather sorry for almost everyone as I drove for the last time along the road to Imunda.

### 21

At six o'clock I reached the jagged signboard.

As I drove over the crest of the plain and the house came into view I looked toward the veranda, hoping to see the truck parked outside, but it was not there.

Luku met me in the yard.

"Where is Bwana Hartleigh?" I asked.

"Left in truck."

"No. Not Bill. Bwana Norman. Bwana Hartleigh."

"Yes. Left in truck."

Luku was staring at me. I forced myself to sound calm and to speak very slowly.

"When, Luku?"

"Not long."

"Then where is the young Bwana?"

"Sijui. Not know. He walk out after he eat. I think he go to shambas, to fields. Then Memsa'ab comes in car. Perhaps he meet car."

"Why do you think so?"

"Because her car stop by wood near shamba . . ."

At last I managed to piece together from what he said a rough sequence of events. After lunch, while Norman was still asleep, Bill had left the house for a walk. About two hours later Mary had arrived in her Ford. Luku had told her that Bill was out and that Norman was still sleeping. Mary had scribbled a quick note on the back of a card, put it in an envelope and handed it to Luku to give Bill on his return. She had then driven away but had stopped for a few minutes by the wood. Tim's boy had arrived half an hour later.

"You're sure the young Bwana has not been back to the house since he left for the shambas?"

"Ndio. Sure."

"Then where are the two letters for him?"

"I put them on the table in big room."

I walked quickly into the sitting room. In daylight the garlands and paper lanterns looked pathetically tawdry. There were no letters on the table. I turned to the desk. Lying on the top of it was a copy of my treatment. Across the title page was written in ink with a firm, clear hand: "In consideration of the sum of one thousand pounds promised me by Stonor Films I give my consent for this film to be made. Norman Hartleigh." Each page was initialed. Pinned to the last page was a check for fifty pounds made out in my name.

Then, in horror, I realized what had happened. When Norman had come into the living room at about five he had seen the two letters addressed to Bill. Tim's envelope was marked "urgent and immediate." Norman had opened it and read the warning. Mary's note would have told him the rest of the story. Norman had immediately taken the truck and driven to the hut.

I walked outside again and found Luku. He was standing in the yard with a troubled expression in his liquid brown eyes. He knew there was something wrong.

"Before Bwana Hartleigh left in the truck, did he ask you any question?"

"He ask if young Bwana meet car later."

"What did you say?"

"Ndio. Yes. Because I see her car stop by wood near shamba."

His answer explained the one thing that had been puzzling me. Norman had therefore presumed – rightly, for all I knew – that Mary had driven Bill to the hut. He had realized, as we had at the Rest House, that the only hope was to reach the hut before darkness.

I looked at the sun, low on the horizon. Within an hour it would be dark, and there was nothing I could do. Then it occurred to me to ask Luku another question.

"Do you know where the hut is, Luku? The hut where the young Bwana drives to near Iringa?"

"Hut, Bwana?"

Luku stared at me, his expression eager yet bewildered, his eyes hopefully questioning me like a spaniel that wants to please his master but does not know what trick he is to perform.

"The small house where he goes. Do you know where it is?"

Luku shook his head sadly.

"No, Bwana."

Bill had been right. Luku knew nothing about it, nor would the girl.

"Thank you, Luku."

I wandered onto the veranda and gazed hopelessly at the declining sun. There was nothing I could now do but wait. As I watched the long shadow creeping over the plain I vaguely noticed a white bird on the near side of the swamp. An instant later I remembered Norman's words: "I see, last of all, his shirt like a white bird fluttering in the distance." I walked to the far end of the veranda and looked again, screening my eyes against the sun. For a while I stared uncertainly. Then I leaped down from the veranda and ran across the garden and stumbled down the slope, waving my arms wildly, rushing toward the man who was climbing up the hillside from the plantation near the swamp. And when he waved his arms in reply and began to run I knew it was Bill.

As we hurried back to the house I told him what had happened. At first Bill was so dazed that he scarcely seemed to understand the words I panted out.

"Norman's driving the truck," he kept repeating.

"How far away is the hut?"

"Thirty miles."

"Is it in open country?"

"There are woods round about."

"Can we get there while it's still light?"

"If we go fast enough."

Neither of us spoke again until we reached my car. We were now oppressed by the same fear. Barry would be hidden, waiting for the truck to approach the hut. He would be certain that Bill was driving. In the darkness he would attack the driver. He might not recognize Norman until too late.

"Can I drive?" Bill asked. "I know the roads."

"Get in then. But I warn you. The road's greasy."

While the car lurched and clattered over the track I looked at Bill. Though he had been running, his face was very white. I could almost feel the effort he was making to appear calm. His lips were drawn into his mouth, his eyes narrowed, his nostrils dilated. Perhaps he had looked thus as he drove his tank toward Caen.

At the turning we branched right – in the direction of Iringa. As soon as we got onto the road I realized that Bill was an excellent driver. He knew the precise moment to brake for a dip; and when the car went into a skid on the sodden surface his hands never faltered. I stopped peering anxiously ahead and began to think about Norman.

I remembered the first night I had dined with him. I had been bored with his stilted, rather forced conversation until – at the very end of the evening – he had begun to speak about what he believed. How did the definition go? "The man won't exert himself in small things because he despises them. But he will run a great risk. And at times of danger he will be reckless of his life." I could recall Norman's tone of voice, quiet, almost awed, as he spoke the truth he had found, and added his own interpretation. "Minor transgressions, the small faults of vanity or lust, can be forgiven. But when the great moment comes, if ever such an opportunity is granted to you in your life, then you must behave impeccably."

I had thought then that his moment had come long ago. I now knew that he had accepted several moments, not only in war but in peace, and at each he had tried to behave perfectly. A few hours previously fate, when he was tired and defeated, had brought him what might perhaps be his last opportunity.

I lit two cigarettes and handed one to Bill.

"Thanks. It's three miles to the turning. And he's not all that far ahead of us judging from the tracks."

The sun was nearly touching the horizon.

"How far is it after the turning?"

"Eight miles. The next three are the worst, though." Bill changed down into second gear. The road now ran along the side of a small escarpment. To our right there was a drop of a hundred feet into the valley.

"God! Why did she have to choose tonight?" Bill said suddenly.

"Opportunity."

"But I'd told her that I wanted to be with Norman tonight."

"Why did Mary stop her car by the wood near one of the plantations?"

"Did she? You never said, but I can tell you why. Before we found the hut we used to meet in that wood by the top shamba."

"How did you discover the hut?"

"I'd gone out to buy some cattle and got lost on my way back. I was going through some woods when I happened to come on the place. It was just an ordinary native hut with a shamba round it that was all overgrown. Obviously the clearing had been given up as a bad job. The hut's roof had fallen in, and some of the wood was rotten, but it was the ideal place for us, and I soon made something out of it."

Bill threw his cigarette out of the window.

"I can't think how he found out where it was," he muttered.

"Perhaps he followed you."

"Maybe."

There was a bend in the road ahead, and Bill slowed down.

"I've been a perfect mug," he said softly.

I was silent, for I could think of no suitable reply.

As we turned the bend, Bill suddenly stamped on the brake pedal. The car swung into a skid and came to rest a yard away from the verge of the escarpment.

"You bloody fool!" I shouted.

I turned to him angrily. Bill was staring straight ahead, his eyes glazed in terror. Then I saw what he was looking at.

Ten yards in front of us, slurred over the muddy red surface of the road, were long skid marks. Further on the tracks ran straight for a few yards as if the car had righted itself. Then the skid marks started again and swerved off to the right. Beyond the road's border the undergrowth had been ripped violently away and a tree snapped near the root. The bared wood gleamed in the fading light.

Bill wrenched open the door of the car and ran up the road to the torn verge and looked down. Then he gave a little cry and began to stumble down the hillside. In cold horror I watched him disappear. The salt taste of fear was in my mouth. But I knew what I would see when I looked down. The time for fear was past.

As I walked unsteadily along the road, an unbidden thought flashed like a jay across the sadness of my mind. "It was the old fool's last opportunity, and he made a mess of it."

I looked down. Far below in the valley I could see the twisted wreck of the truck. I began to clamber down the steep hillside, clutching at the roots of trees to save myself from falling, dislodging stones that clattered against the huge boulders, slithering over the patches of damp soil.

It seemed a long time before I reached the valley.

A few yards away from the overturned truck, Bill was leaning over Norman's broken, dead body.

He was crying bitterly. His grief rent the stillness of the evening as he rocked to and fro in an anguish of despair. For an instant he looked up at me through his tears, then he lowered his head. He was saying something, repeating the same phrase over and over again, but the words were stifled by the sobs that choked him. I knelt down and tried to comfort him. And as I knelt I heard the words that he was crying.

"He was an old bastard. But I loved him, I loved him."

## PART III

Wanda had driven me to Soho Square on her way to a rehearsal.

I was a few minutes early for the conference so I stopped in the outer office to see Miss Agnew, Stonor's personal secretary.

"You're quite a stranger. You've been away a long time," she said.

"Only two months."

I noticed that her smile revealed fewer teeth than usual. Perhaps my small prestige was waning.

"How are things?" I asked brightly.

"Not too bad, but we've been pretty busy with 'The Crimson Doll.' Sir Louis leaves for New York tomorrow."

"What's he doing there?"

Miss Agnew assumed her discreetly knowing expression.

"Some business deal," she said, and looked up at the clock. "You'd better be going in or you'll get the sack," she laughed.

Her laugh sounded to me a little forced. I walked into the long white and gilt room feeling vaguely uneasy.

They were all there – even Drake. I wondered why he had been summoned. Calmann lumbered toward me and put a heavy arm around my shoulder.

"Welcome back, David," he said. "We missed you. My wife hopes you dine with us tomorrow night."

"I'd love to."

"You've heard the news, I suppose?" Roy Nixon said.

A hothouse carnation was wilting in his buttonhole. Both of them had probably had a tiring day.

"I don't expect so."

"M.T.A. have started a film about Moira Blane. That bitches us completely. A famous actress. Almost the same period. I'm afraid we've had to shelve the Daphne Moore project indefinitely."

"Good."

"We thought you'd be disappointed," Desmond Arles said.

His blue velvet tie brought out the color of his close-set eyes. He was wearing a new pair of suède boots. Otherwise he did not appear to have changed.

"There are other stories ready to be made," I said.

"There are," Desmond agreed. "But quite frankly, we've got nothing up your street just at present. In fact, I don't really know what there is for you to do right now."

Then I saw the danger. My contract was due to be renewed in a month's time.

"What about my Tanganyika story?"

Roy's nose gave a little twitch.

"We're not absolutely happy about it, David," he said. "The background stuff's all right, but the story itself is a bit too simple."

"You said you wanted a vehicle for Dick Calpe and Judy Grant. They can get across about as much subtlety as a couple of rhinos."

"All the same . . ." Desmond began.

Suddenly Roy sprang to his feet. The door at the far end of the room had been flung open, and Stonor was advancing toward us across the thick red carpet.

"Hullo, Dave!" he said. "I'm glad you weren't savaged by lions."

When he shook my hand heartily my heart sank. Long experience had taught me that his effusiveness heralded disaster.

"You had quite a pleasant little trip at our expense," he said with a smile as he sat down behind his huge telephone-laden desk.

"Delightful."

His eye focused on me for a moment, then swiveled to the notes on his desk.

"Now, gentlemen, first we must dispose of the Daphne Moore project," he said. "As you may have heard, Dave, we've decided for various reasons not to go ahead with it. That brings me to the question of costs. The board doesn't question your salary and expenses, Dave. They can be set against a Tanganyika story – if we can find a satisfactory one."

Stonor paused. I knew that the board existed in name only. Stonor used the term "board" as a polite pseudonym for the part of him that was concerned with hard cash.

"Now we come to the question of this payment of a thousand pounds for permission to use Norman Hartleigh's character on the screen," Stonor continued. "I gather from our legal department that Hartleigh gave this permission shortly before his unfortunate accident. Is that so, Dave?"

"Yes."

"What proof is there of that?"

"His writing and signature on the treatment itself."

"Was there any witness to that signature?"

"Not that I know of."

"Then wasn't it rather presumptuous of you to pay out the money without consulting our legal department?"

"We had offered him one thousand pounds for his permission. The legal department confirmed it in writing. He accepted our offer – also in writing. It never occurred to me that it was anything but a clear contract."

"Drake, what is your view?"

Drake unclasped his hands.

"On the face of it I would suppose that Mr. Brent's view was correct."

Stonor frowned.

"Very well. I can only say that it seems to me that the affair was unfortunately handled. What's the point of paying out a thousand pounds to a man who's dead?" he asked impatiently.

"I paid the money to his estate."

"Who does that benefit – apart from a bunch of lawyers?"

Drake winced and folded his hands quickly.

"The beneficiary under the terms of his will."

"Who was that?"

"A man called Wayne."

"What's he done to deserve it? Anyhow, the matter seems beyond our control now, and we mustn't waste any more time. Drake, I know you're a busy man, so I expect you'd like to go."

"Thank you," Drake said, and walked reverently out of the room with the delicate, short steps of a choirboy retiring to the vestry.

"Now let's come to your Tanganyika story," Stonor said. "I appreciate that you were writing it as a vehicle for Calpe and Grant, but I must confess I was disappointed. I couldn't *see* the characters, and the plot was far too simple. I'm afraid it wasn't up to your usual standard."

"I'm sorry. But with those actors I thought you wanted a straightforward action picture."

"The public taste is changing, Dave. They're getting tired of the cops and robbers type of film. They want the real thing, stark and unvarnished – so far as censorship will allow, of course. They want true-to-life characters – not forced into the story. That's the kind of picture I'm determined to make.

That's the kind of script I want written. Have you any ideas, Dave?"

"None at present."

"After all, you were out there two months. You must have come across *something* exciting. Take Hartleigh's accident. A man drives his car over a precipice. Why? Was he drunk? Was he distracted? Did he want to kill himself? Why did that accident occur?"

"Because he was a bad driver and the road was greasy."

Stonor suppressed a gesture of annoyance.

"I must warn you, Dave, that at present we've got no story ready for you to work on. You must understand that."

I understood well enough. In other words, unless I produced a story quickly my contract would not be renewed.

Stonor smiled at me hopefully.

"You've been thinking along cops and robbers lines," he explained. "Think again while Desmond is telling us his new story."

Stonor turned toward Desmond.

"If you're ready, Desmond," he said. "No. Put away those notes. I want you to tell us the story in your own words."

Desmond uncrossed his legs, smiled around the room with the correct degree of modesty, and began a story about a boy whose love for his pony brought his two estranged parents together. There was nothing new about it. He had told it to me at least three times.

While Desmond talked I tried to think of a stark unvarnished story that would pass the censor, but my mind went blank. I cursed Stonor for giving me such impossibly short notice. Then I tried to think of the people I had met in Tanganyika. Arising from their lives, what uncensorable story could I invent? What could I devise from the Aruna types?

My mind skipped away from the immediate problem, and I began to wonder what was happening to them all now. What was Bill doing at this precise moment?

It was six o'clock – nine in Tanganyika. Bill would have

finished his evening meal. He was probably sitting in an armchair between the two sibilant lamps in the sitting room. He
was probably alone. Luku would be in the boys' quarters, and
Halima had gone back to her tribe. Norman had left her a
hundred pounds. She was now an heiress who could afford to
choose the man she fancied.

One thing was certain. Mary would not be there with Bill,
for the affair had ended the night that Norman died.

Bill and I had been unable to move the body up the steep
hillside without help. I had therefore driven into Iringa to tell
the police about the accident and to fetch boys and ropes.
Bill had remained to keep vigil, for the body could not be
left. The vultures were already gathering. I had returned two
hours after dark with some askaris and a sergeant. While the
body was being raised Barry had driven up in his car.

When Barry saw the group in the road he stopped and
switched on the inside light. Mary was sitting beside him. She
had been crying. I found out later that Barry had grown tired
of waiting and had broken into the hut and found her alone.
There had been a violent quarrel, and in the end Mary had
won.

But I knew nothing of their reconciliation and of Barry's
passionate promise to mend his ways when I walked up to
their car and told them about the accident. Mary shud-
dered and buried her face in her hands. Barry neither spoke
nor moved. His face was raised toward me in a look of dis-
dain. I felt he was observing my emotion with contempt.
As I looked at his arrogant brown eyes and thick lips, I lost
control, and the words poured out of my mouth. Murderer,
sadist, braggart – I no longer cared what I said. I only hoped
that he would leap out of the car and attack me so that I could
return force with violence. Yet part of me disowned the stam-
mering words spurting out into the night.

Barry listened to me in silence. When he spoke his quiet
voice made me ashamed of my outburst.

"You may be right," he said, "but don't forget that I'm not
the only one to blame."

Then I realized I had mistaken his dismay for conceit.

"Is there anything we can do here to help?"

Immediately I noticed his use of the word "we."

"Nothing now."

"I don't expect we'll see you again out here," he said. "Mary's taking me back to England."

Mary took her hands away from her smeared face.

"Tell Bill – tell Bill not to worry about me," she said in a low, trembling voice. "Tell him Barry's promised – no, that's not fair – just tell him that it's going to be all right. Good-bye, David. And thanks for your help."

Barry waved his hand and they drove away.

So Bill would probably be alone with the lamps and his thoughts in the house that now belonged to him.

And that got me no further with my story, nor did their past set-up.

Desmond was tracing elegant designs with his hand in the air. His voice vibrated with pent-up emotion. He must be reaching the end of his tale. I listened.

"Then we have a three-shot of the boy and his father and mother standing outside the ranch house," Desmond was saying. "And we know that they will never part again."

Desmond smoothed back his hair nervously and sat back in his chair.

"Gentlemen, I would like your comments," Stonor said.

Roy Nixon's nose began to twitch nervously.

"It's good," he said. "But there's not much passion in it."

Irrelevantly I wondered how much passion Mrs. Nixon found in bed.

"Ronnie Burke would be just perfect for the boy," Eddie Roach suggested eagerly.

"I thought Ronnie Burke got into trouble for seducing a girl under age," Stonor said.

"Yes, he did," Eddie agreed, unabashed. "But he can still play down to twelve or thirteen, and he's a fine little actor."

"André, how do you like the story?" Stonor asked.

Calmann opened his eyes.

"I always think it has possibilities," he said in his deep gut-tural voice. "I made it in 1926."

There was an awkward silence. Stonor looked at his watch.

"All the best stories have been used before," he said. "The time's getting on. Any other business?"

"What about David's story?" Roy asked.

Roy was not an unkind person. When he gave me his nursery-governess look I knew that he meant: "This is your last chance if you want your contract renewed."

Stonor turned toward me.

"Have you racked your brain?"

"Yes."

"Any results so far?"

Part of me longed to tell Stonor just what I thought of him. Yet he was neither villain nor fool. At least he gave his directors the chance to make a good film.

"Any results so far?" he repeated.

"Some," I said. But I was only playing for time.

"You needn't go into details. Just give us the rough theme."

"Can't David be given a week?" Calmann asked.

"I leave for New York tomorrow. You know I won't be back for two weeks. Just give me an outline, David. I can judge from that."

I was silent. Stonor's gaze swam away from me toward Roy.

"Give me the circuit figures for the last week, Roy. There's something I must check."

Roy began to fumble in his pigskin dispatch case.

I had got a few minutes' respite. But other worries now came tumbling through my mind. . . . The prospect was grim. I might get a job in another studio, but with hundreds of scriptwriters unemployed it would be difficult. I had saved little money. I had been so sure of myself that I had never considered the possibility that my contract might not be renewed. I might get a job as an assistant in a scenario depart-ment – the hardest hack work, writing synopses of every bright novel that appeared. I *must* find a story. There must be one buried below the level of my consciousness.

Then, suddenly, the idea swept over me. It was so obvious that I chided myself for not seeing it before. It had been staring me in the face for weeks, crying out to be used.

I must improvise the changes quickly. One character had to be suppressed, others created, two modified. Then I must change all the names, and I was there, home and dry.

It was quite simple. I would use – not my bogus treatment – but the real story of Daphne Moore and Norman as the basis. In my version, when he went down to stay with Daphne, Norman would be wildly attracted by a young servant girl of seventeen who worked in the house. The girl would fall passionately in love with him. Daphne would discover the truth and stage the scene in the hall to humiliate him. Bill, sweet stupid Bill Wayne, would in 1950 be the offspring of the union between Norman and the girl. (The dates could be adjusted to fit.) But Bill would not know the reason why Norman had sought him out and adopted him. The story flowed naturally from there. I would have to change the characters of Mary and Barry. I would have to change part of the plot. But certainly in the end Norman would sacrifice himself for his son. Though it presented various censorship difficulties, it was a good film story.

I was about to speak when a picture of Norman slid into my mind. He was sitting in his armchair in the sitting room, glass in hand, wearing his shiny blue suit. "He won't run risks for small ends," he was saying. "He won't exert himself in small things, because he despises them."

"But why should he despise small things?" I cried inwardly to this ghost. "We live day by day. It's the small things we have to deal with, whether we like it or not – the small rather dull matters, not the great. To hell with great moments! If they come our way we'll try to behave well. But meanwhile there's today to think of and tomorrow. We have to earn money and eat food and sleep somewhere. We have to deal with tinkers and tailors and the Sir Louis Stonors of life.

"I'm not a man of great mind. I've never pretended to be – not even to myself. I'm a plain laborer who happens to work with a pen, not a shovel. I'm a hack at the bottom of the cavern of this world. Here is the life that is real to me – here in this very room, all around me. You could afford to cling to your values; I can't. And you mustn't blame me."

As I looked up at Stonor he put down the report.

"Well, Dave?" he asked.

"I think I've got it," I said.

Perhaps he heard the suppressed excitement in my voice, for he stretched out for the green telephone and took up the receiver.

"I'll be late," he said. "Tell them to start without me."

Then his gaze floated slowly toward me.

"Are you going to tell us the theme or the story?"

"The whole works."

"Take your time, Dave. Just tell it in your own words."

I tried to suppress the silly waves of panic that came surging over me. I tried to banish the picture of the gray-haired man in his shabby suit. I cleared my throat and took a deep breath. Here we go again, I thought.

"The main action of the story takes place in Tanganyika," I began. "But there's one flashback to England. The film opens with a young journalist coming out . . ."

"I want you to make me *see* what happens," Stonor interrupted quietly. "And if I can really see it, then we'll make it that way."

The familiar words dispelled the last traces of Norman from my mind.

"A young journalist coming out from England to interview a famous painter," I continued in a firm voice, happy now that I had come back to reality, happy now that I was home again.

Printed in August 2021
by Rotomail Italia S.p.A., Vignate (MI) - Italy